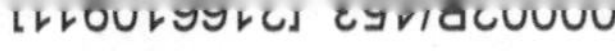

About Rob Couteau:

Positive reviews of Rob Couteau's books have appeared in the *Midwest Book Review*, *Publishers Weekly Select*, and Barney Rosset's *Evergreen Review*. In 1985 he won the North American Essay Award, a competition sponsored by the American Humanist Association. His work as a critic, interviewer, and social commentator has been featured in books such as *Gabriel Garcia Marquez's 'Love in the Time of Cholera'* by Thomas Fahy, *Conversations with Ray Bradbury* edited by Steven Aggelis, *Ghetto Images in Twentieth-Century American Literature* by Tyrone R. Simpson, and David Cohen's *Forgotten Millions*, a book about the homeless mentally ill. Over one-hundred selections of his poetry and prose have appeared in over forty-five periodicals. Couteau's interviews include conversations with Ray Bradbury, Pulitzer Prize-winning author Justin Kaplan, *Last Exit to Brooklyn* novelist Hubert Selby, Simon & Schuster editor Michael Korda, LSD discoverer Dr. Albert Hofmann, Picasso's model and muse Sylvette David, Nabokov biographer Robert Roper, music producer Danny Goldberg, poet and publisher Ed Foster, and historian Philip Willan, author *Puppetmasters: The Political Use of Terrorism in Italy*.

In the early 1980s, Couteau worked as a client advocate in the New York City mental health system. Employed initially as a case manager and subsequently as a director for a community residence program, he was tasked with insuring that the patients' civil rights were protected. *Doctor Pluss* is the fictionalized account that emerged from those years of intensive advocacy work, which often involved serving as a liaison between patients and mental health practitioners such as social workers, psychologists, and psychiatrists. It portrays a milieu in which the road to hell is paved with psychiatric good intentions.

Critical acclaim for *Doctor Pluss*:

Rob Couteau describes *Doctor Pluss* as "... fiction based on actual dialogues with schizophrenic patients, diabolically 'sane' psychotherapists, and well-meaning yet unerringly destructive social workers. It chronicles the descent of an eccentric, sardonic, and witty psychiatrist into what appears to be a state of complete madness."

His intention to metaphorically and realistically portray and contrast the madness of psychiatric process as well as its patients is powerfully wrought in a story about patients "surviving this holocaust of forgetfulness." During this process, their identities and personalities are lost in the institutional morass of a center purported to excel in rehabilitation, but which actually contains many ethical and personal challenges to the new psychiatric resident at the Walt Whitman Asylum for Adults, Dr. Pluss.

It's a place of rage and despair, of ambiguity where hope and horror run close together, and daily gives Dr. Pluss pause for thought about his patients and his role in their lives: "In her own unwitting way, Pluss mused, Evelyn personified the dual aspects of the godhead: horror and joy; awe and fascination."

Novellas typically are hard-hitting but often artificially succinct in their brevity. Often, one is left wanting for more. The best of them (of which *Doctor Pluss* is one) excels in taking this succinctness to its most logical conclusion, creating slices of life which are narrow enough to receive full-bodied flavor as the plot and characters develop.

One does not wish for more in *Doctor Pluss*. It's complete unto itself, exceptionally well developed, and emotionally compelling, connecting metaphorical description with experiences that often challenge the traditional roles of doctor and patient, linking them in unexpected ways.

Each patient has their own special struggle with perceptions and illusions that influence reality. Rob Couteau's descriptions are often long and detailed, demanding a slower, more contemplative reading style than is usual in novels in general and novellas in particular. These long sentences are packed with description that grabs heart and mind: "It was tragically convenient to blame her uncontrollable obesity and fierce primal appetite upon this crazy cat of the fleshy sphinx, this lazy Egyptian feline entombed within, lost in a drifting, timeless time of metempsychosis and crocodile gods, of the loopy eye of the *ankh* – a cross with a teardrop on top – mystic symbol for who knows what. Into the loop one entered and never again returned, adrift with the sacred crocodiles and lost in a thick bed of reeds asway in a warm, mosquito breeze, the muddy Nile lapping you along to your mother's teat which is the grand fan of the delta: lush black earth of Moses and Nefertiti and Alexander and Akhenaton, all had wet themselves in her deltoid lap – let me wash you clean with my dirty waters and raise your material soul to a vast glittering realm of *death, death, death* – great Egyptian fantasy that delivered us to Hades, where we left this paltry life of the living and gladly marched to the everlasting realm of the deceased."

Run-on sentence, or beautiful metaphor for a mental condition? Couteau is not afraid to push the literary boundaries of convention in pursuit of a different form of descriptive truth, bringing readers along in a rollicking ride through schizophrenic experience that ultimately questions the foundations of reality and perception from both sides of the therapist's couch.

His interpretations and descriptions of the schizophrenic experience are particularly astute, astonishing, and evocatively described.

When Pluss vanishes, a ripple of effects on doctors and patients alike threatens to change everything. A regression process takes place that questions both convention and traditional roles.

Readers who choose *Doctor Pluss* are in for a treat. It's like *One Flew Over the Cuckoo's Nest* on steroids: a thought-provoking examination of sanity, insanity, and the crossover process that leaves readers thinking long after this therapeutic slice of life is consumed.
– Diane Donovan, *Midwest Book Review* (April 2020).

* * *

Amazingly beautiful, haunting prose. It's a great book.
– Christopher Sawyer-Lauçanno, author of *The Continual Pilgrimage: American Writers in Paris* (City Lights), *An Invisible Spectator: A Biography of Paul Bowles* (Grove Press).

* * *

Intellectual freshness, richness, and potency ... Couteau is an impressively creative writer, whom Barney Rosset urged me to review.
– Jim Feast, assistant editor of the *Evergreen Review*.

ROB COUTEAU

Doctor Pluss

With an Afterword
by Jim Feast

DOMINANTSTAR

Dominantstar, New York.

This book is a work of fiction. Names, characters, places, and incidents either are products of the author's imagination or are used fictitiously. Any resemblance to actual events, locales, or persons, living or dead, is entirely coincidental.

Third, revised edition. 1 2 3 4 5 6 7 8 9 10 01

The second chapter of *Doctor Pluss* appeared in *Hawaii Pacific Review* under the title "Sublunary Delights." Chapter 3, "Portrait of a Cat Remedy," was featured in *Rockhurst Review* and in *Psychological Poems: Journal of Outsider Poetry*. Other excerpts were published in *Croton Review* and *Z Miscellaneous*.

Thanks to Jim Lampos and Carolyn Montgomery of Rupert Crew, Ltd.

This edition is dedicated to Marge Couteau.

Cover: *Seated Woman*, oil on canvas, by Rob Couteau.

Dominantstar LLC:
dominantstarpublications.com

Author's web site:
robcouteau.com

Paperback ISBN 978-0-9966888-6-4
E-book ISBN 978-0-9966888-8-8

He was seen knocking on doors that concealed those who no longer materialized from the squalid shadows: patients who ceased to witness the phenomenon of sunlight and who were fused into a web of dust and grime that shaped the contours of their forgotten chambers. Patients who, once upon a time, had been catalogued in a case note that was afterward misplaced, thereby causing said patient to be misplaced; and, thus, doctor, when the ink on the case notes fades I, too, will fade away; and the patients vanished, and no one was aware of their loss or mourned their absence. And when the files were placed in the wrong folders, the patients switched identities; and when the notes were crumpled or discarded the patients were themselves crushed – and liberated – by death. Of the ones surviving this holocaust of forgetfulness were those with skin so pale and rid of pigmentation that the doctor had developed a special theory proposing that, in a former life, they'd belonged to an esoteric genus of albino bottom dwellers: pink pulpous androgyns unsexed by an absolute darkness and blinded when removed from that drear pitch: a bobbing, hovering school of gelatinous moonbeams with hazy albugo eyes that cut faint traces across the black waters of a perpetual night.

— "The Analysis," from *Doctor Pluss*

Diffuse light filtered through soiled curtains, illuminating the patients' gaunt faces. Seated haphazardly in metal folding chairs, they sipped bitter coffee from paper cups. Several whispered to themselves; others gazed solemnly at the floor.

Dr. Pluss nodded to a group of shabbily dressed men gathered round a table. One grinned childishly into his cup, which he clutched with large waxen hands.

"Plussa! Plussa! Come'ere! *Come'ere!*"

As soon as Anna Jones had spotted him, she bellowed out his name. Her pleas were urgent and desperate, as if something terrible had just occurred. But Pluss had encountered her in this state so many times before that he knew better than to panic.

Anna greeted him with an exaggerated grin, her lips gleaming with abundant polish. Her pigtails, tied with red and blue ribbons, flopped back and forth as she rocked mechanically in her chair. A chalky pink powder coated her face, and rouged circles were drawn on each cheek. Black-button eyes added to her clownish look, as did the extra-large clothing of incongruous styles draped round her massive frame. The lapels of her blouse were riddled with rows of colored safety pins that she haughtily displayed like an array of military medals accrued in the aftermath of some honorably fought engagement.

"Anna Banana," Pluss playfully called, "what is it, what is it?"

Now she grew even more animated, the ribbons quivering with each ungainly jerk of her head.

"Plussa, Plussa! I need a pencil, *I need a pencil!*"

"But, Anna, you already have fifty million pencils! What do you need another pencil for?"

"*A ha-ha-ha-ha-ha-ha!* Plussa, Plussa, stop it, stop it!

You're killing me; you're killing me! *A ha-ha-ha-ha-ha!* Come on, gimme a pencil, *gimme a pencil!*"

Pluss dramatically reached into his suit jacket to retrieve a pencil that he'd removed from the art-supplies room earlier that day, having anticipated that he would encounter her later on.

"Here you go, Anna."

"Oh, thanks'a, thanks'a ..." She carefully appraised it, then added it to her collection.

"And what about a safety pin?"

"But, Anna, you already have a hundred million safety pins."

"Plussa, stop it, stop it, you're too funny; you're too funny! *A ha-ha-ha-ha-ha!*"

After allowing her to catch her breath, he asked, "Listen, Anna, have you seen Tanya?"

"Tanya, the case manager?"

"Yes, Tanya."

"Oh, yeah, I know Tanya!" Pointing toward a corridor, she shouted, "Other community room! And tell 'em to stop smoking!" Anna repeatedly jabbed her finger at a tall thin man huddled beneath a tattered hat at the far end of the room. "Stop smoking!" Her body trembled, the loose flesh of her forearms jiggling as she shook her fists. "Filthy bastards!"

As if emerging from a trance, the man suddenly turned and shouted, "Shut up, you fat fuck!"

"No good, filthy bastards," Anna sighed. "They kill me with their smoke. I no like it, Dr. Pluss. You gotta do something, because they're *filthy fucks*, doctor. I got so mad, I threw a chair and *brok'a da mirror ...*"

As if admiring her handiwork, Anna turned to a wall-length mirror and grinned at the widening fractures of glass, which surrounded her like a glinting web.

"That's quite a job, Anna. You know, you have talents that I've never even noticed before."

"*A ha-ha-ha-ha-ha!* Plussa, get outta here!"

As he turned to leave, Anna sighed: "*Ooooo*-kay. But you sure you ain't got no safety pin?"

Pluss considered the final community room to be the gloomiest and most desolate of all. Perhaps it was because something more had been expected from this site, designated as the place where each case manager would entertain their patients with so-called *rehabilitative activities*. Here, they would fashion a variety of educational seminars: cute little tidbits tossed into a harrowing void left in the wake of a schizophrenic episode.

And now, as resident psychiatrist, even Dr. Pluss was obliged to design a few of these therapy groups. He shuddered to recall the personnel director gleefully noting his past career in the visual arts and how he had then requested, all to the doctor's horror, that he assume command of the already in progress, weekly arts-and-crafts group.

The counselor who was originally in charge had instructed the patients to construct little wooden houses from popsicle sticks. Each member had received a simple set of diagrams and an ample supply of glue and sticks. Then, the following week, the responsibility for the class had been passed on to the doctor.

But instead of building houses, Pluss had purchased paper, paints, and brushes and, upon his arrival, he calmly instructed the patients to dispose of their silly popsicle-stick kits. They obeyed him unquestioningly, but not without first pausing to consider the perplexed expression of their former counselor, who appeared to be as bewildered as they were as the sticks fluttered into a large steel drum and Pluss commanded everyone – *to paint!*

But *what* should they paint? they asked. Paint anything! Pluss exclaimed. But the patients remained immobile, some sitting with bowed heads, others staring blankly. But I *can't* paint, said one. And I don't know *what* to paint, protested another. But everyone can paint! Pluss retorted. Then *you* show us what to paint, doctor. No, Pluss calmly continued, I am the master; you, the pupils. And I'm here to inform you that everyone has within them thousands, hundreds of thousands, millions, billions of images! Each of us contains a veritable alphabet of paint! Each a unique manner of expression! And I will guide you; I will direct your creative spirit. A spirit that *demands* its day on earth ..."

An idea, someone whined, give us an idea! Pluss glanced round, then snatched a stack of magazines from a nearby table. Here, each of you, grab a magazine, tear out an image, and *interpret* it! You mean paint it, Dr. Pluss? Yes, in your own way – bring it to life!

He flipped open a magazine to a glossy advertisement: three sad-eyed dachshunds sitting on a brightly waxed kitchen floor, their droopy faces transfixed on the silent patients.

Look at this! What a silly image! Now, bring this dead bunch of mutts to life!

After another pause, Dora Washington volunteered: All right, Dr. Pluss. I'll bring them mutts back from the grave. You can't expect me to be no Rembrandt, but I'll try!

Dora opened her watercolor kit and stared solemnly at the miniature paint wafers. She slowly dipped a brush into water, flicked it across a pigment, then let it stream along the absorbent paper.

As the colors blossomed upon the composition, the other patients gradually discarded their apprehension, and soon everyone was painting. Thanks to Dora's courage, Pluss had succeeded in winning them over. The following week, in his premier *Hamlet* class, he again cultivated the interest of a select group of schizophrenics as he expounded, with animated zeal, on Hamlet's bizarre inability to *kill the king*.

A high-pitched voice interrupted his reverie: "Everyone, thanks for coming!"

At the far end of the community room, Tanya was addressing a small group seated at a table.

"Today, class, we have a special guest," she smiled as her lingering gaze focused on the doctor, "who will briefly lecture about one of *his* favorite artists."

Pluss gasped: he'd forgotten all about it! Tanya had asked him to make a presentation, but it had completely slipped his mind.

As he approached the table, he nodded politely to each of them:

"Dora. Monroe. Alexandria. Diana. Yes, today, I'd like to share with you my passionate appreciation of the Swiss painter, Paul Klee. Tanya, do you have the illustration that we discussed earlier?" As the class shifted their attention to Tanya, he nodded discreetly at her art-history book.

She quickly scanned the pages, frantically searching for a Klee reproduction. Since they'd never engaged in any such discussion, he'd have to improvise. Meanwhile, he wondered what he might conjure about the hermetic painter from Switzerland.

Well, for starters, Klee was a native of *Bern*: a name with gravitas, but a place he knew nothing about. He envisioned a Chagall-like rendering of a medieval European hamlet: crooked rows of houses scattered beneath a panorama of twinkling stars. The streets emptied of everything but an animated trio of red cockatoos, ambling upon a winding mustard-colored road. The birds waggled with big burdensome wings: feathers of alizarin, silvered under a glowering moon. During the day, they remained listless: fat frowzy birdbrains, shiftless and slovenly. While the squat vegetable-stall vendors crouched hard at work over their rickety carts, snarling and cursing beneath floppy felt fedoras, their fob-watch ticktock pockets adorned with redbird appliqués, the wings silver-tipped and neatly pasted upon each ragged lapel …

"Yes, it's here, doctor." Fortunately, she'd found one. As she passed him the book, he recognized it at once: *Lost in Thought*, a lithograph from 1917.

"Ah, here we go, *Lost in Thought*! One of my favorites, which is why I selected it for study today. So that I might share with you my thoughts concerning this evocative rendition of the human visage: of the stately persona of the artist as he gazes inward, removed from the skirmishes of the annoying, distracting, and unimportant (to him!) outside universe. Yes, I know that many of you oftentimes feel this way: locked in or locked out; shut in or shut out; or in some manner excluded from the daily comings and goings of the ten-thousand-and-some-odd things that we refer to as *reality*."

Monroe raised his hand, but Pluss cut him short:

"Oh, no; don't ask '*What is reality?*' Monroe. But do consider Klee. Did he care to participate in the slaughter, the ennui, the multitude of barbarities? Of course not. Klee had bigger fish to fry. He had his watercolors! His nature studies! His crayons! Even his paint-by-number kits, just like us. And instead of raising a dozen kids, there were a dozen pale canvases all waiting patiently – vistas of beauty that didn't moan, that didn't whine or wail, that didn't so much as *peekaboo*. A dozen epiphanies! And for each of his dozen creations, at least ten dozen inspirations!"

At first, Pluss hid the image from the class. Holding the book against his chest, he'd occasionally glance down, as if it might engender an inspired phrase.

"But *what* did he paint, Dr. Pluss?" Monroe finally blurted out.

"Ah, yes, Monroe, a very sensible inquiry. That *crazy* Swiss! He painted watches! No, no; only joking, Monroe. Well, he composed slithering golden-eyed serpents; crimson weather balloons floating upside down; ferocious felines with incandescent orange fur; tiny blue men with oversized heads and burdened with weighty ideas; lost little girls in monstrous green meadows; medieval castles aglitter and electric; sun-bleached minarets pierced with tar-black Arabian smiles; and everything and anything a mad Swiss with buggy caveman eyes *would* conceivably paint."

Trying to suppress a smile, Tanya's expression contorted, then broke into an odd, Picasso-like grimace: half-smiling, half-grave.

"Can we see one? Can we see a Paul Klee castle? A Paul Klee masterpiece?"

"Well, my dear Monroe, I do not have a castle. But I have something even better, something far more striking!" Now he turned the book round for all to see. "Yes, here, class, is the most dazzling self-portrait ever produced – at least in my humble opinion. Notice the brutal elegance of this etching, so appropriately entitled, *Lost in Thought*."

As the class gaped at the small reproduction, Pluss was finally chagrined by their silence. When he turned to Tanya, she belatedly attempted to squelch her laughter, which now resembled the squeal of a rapidly deflating balloon.

"Yes," he continued, undaunted. "It is stupefying. And I can see that you are, quite understandably, stupefied! No matter. Let this odd hieroglyph sink in. Permit it a chance to penetrate, to pry into your deepest reaches. Yes, class: *Lost in Thought* ..."

Despite their reserve, Pluss was particularly fond of these particular patients. As they solemnly pondered the print, he regarded them tenderly:

First, he was drawn to Dora, who tightly gripped a pencil as if awaiting instruction. He wondered why she was so content, rarely appearing distraught. With her mental and physical disability (because of a birth defect, her right hand bore only two fingers), there was much to challenge her sense of well-being.

Then he regarded Alexandria, a diminutive African lady who believed that she was a man. She would greet the day with a swaggering, rough-and-tumble manner, shoving past the other patients with her brow furrowed, as if eternally angered, and with her lithe figure molded with a cast-iron resolve. Day after day, she strutted about with a mechanical gait. But he'd once espied her alone in her room, prancing before a mirror while garbed in a lacey white dress.

And then there was the mystery of Diana, with her hunched over frame and meek, darting glance. Plagued with bouts of severe paranoia, she would sequester herself alone in her room and remain there, isolated for days at a time. It was difficult to imagine her as the same woman who had surprised everyone with such uncanny artistic talent. After he'd constructed a *nature morte,* Diana had focused her flinty gaze upon the vase, fruits, and flowers; then she attacked the canvas with a startling vengeance. Pluss regarded her as a metaphysical painter of a previously unexplored style. Instead of portraying milky white jugs floating in vaporous haze, Diana stunned the viewer with a portrait of the abyss that was as striking as any great primitive art, yet as magically wistful as the finest Morandi.

Finally, there was Monroe, with his average build; average face; and gray, average way of conversing, of carrying himself rather blandly through every conceivable situation. Yet nothing average about his tender gaze, which resembled that of a child struck with wonder.

And how to account for his peculiar symptom? For Monroe claimed to detect odors that, objectively speaking, didn't exist. Often, they were simple, mundane fragrances, such as when Monroe's blanket had hosted an imaginary mildew. Such a banal innocent delusion and, thus, so befitting Monroe!

But what did it all mean? What was the nose attempting to articulate through such archaic symbols? There was another odd quirk: something in the way that Monroe dressed reminded Pluss of a gas-station attendant. He imagined him in a deep-blue mechanic's uniform, donning a baseball cap and wiping grease from his hands with a coarse white towel. Wiping and smiling until Pluss also smelled the evaporated gasoline, until Pluss likewise yearned to be lifted to such sweet, olfactory heights of wide-nostriled delight.

As he continued to contemplate this small group

assembled at the table, Pluss considered himself lucky: blessed, indeed, to have such a captive audience! Perhaps it was a sign:

The Sign of Four,

a mystery fit for Conan Doyle, himself a doctor.

But the fates had cast them into this wretched, sullen, stench-filled hovel. No wonder Monroe hallucinated with his nose. Perhaps, he might work something into the lecture – a theme to assist Monroe in his quest.

"Class," he continued, "this powerful rendition is not simply the image of someone withdrawn from the world. Rather, it portrays a man experiencing the *inner world.* The emphasis is so much on the world within that the outer facade has begun to transform into a strange medley of shapes, signs, and symbols.

"For we see that Klee has fashioned the nose to resemble a medical study, with the tip neatly severed to reveal a fresh perspective to the anatomy student. Perhaps the incision was due more to an aesthetic decision than to anything else; for, had the tip remained anatomically intact, it would appear to penetrate the external world. Instead, it remains flat: devoid of any classical perspective, and a wonderful device for conveying the relativity of space. This ability to imply an essential reality while simultaneously appearing two-dimensional is real magic, and was perhaps inspired by the wondrous Persian miniatures that so skillfully employ this same technique."

Pluss paused to glance at Monroe, who scratched his nostrils with an almost frenzied gesture.

"Regarding the nose, it is, after all, a symbolic one. In its flatness it remains primal in appearance, like a pig's snout, thus alluding to a primitive, instinctive reality. Such primeval power is echoed in precisely rendered lines of tension, which rise up in waves to the area above and between the eyes, where an accented central line marks a climax of unnerving inner stress. The tightly closed eyelids wrinkle in tense, cresting waves of agitation. The vertical lines above the nose swell, like small lungs inhaling a doleful air, while the lips appear cracked: lacerated with vertical stripes and emphasizing a tightly drawn, pained, forcibly stilled meditation."

Pluss closed his eyes and paced in lengthy strides beside the wall. He only half-understood whatever it was he was espousing, yet intuitively he felt on track, logical, decisive. He took a deep breath, then continued:

"The overall feel of this bust resembles that of a well-shined bell: one grand and immobile, yet about to swing into clamorous revolt. The expression is highly symmetrical, reflecting an inner psychic symmetry fixed between two opposites: one seeking calm, the other about to explode."

At that moment, Monroe let go a loud fart. Pluss opened his eyes to observe Dora pinching her nostrils. He pretended not to notice, closed his eyes, and concluded:

"The most remarkable thing about this portrayal of the self is that it seems to offer nothing to the world, yet all the world may stop to receive as great a transformation through this image as through any other significant vision. Although the world has lost its obsessive attraction for this man, we feel as if we are being pulled by an alluring gravity into him. With a handful of such masterly lines, Klee has achieved all this. His portrait is, like most of his work, a rendition not of the ego but of the greater self that propels mankind."

When he opened his eyes, Pluss found himself standing at the entrance to the room. A crowd of patients had gathered in the hallway and was clapping excitedly. Even Anna had abandoned her haunt beside the splintered mirror to witness the event. When she caught his glance, she shouted:

"Plussa, Plussa! *Ooooo*-kay!"

Confused by the excitement, he searched for Tanya. He hadn't noticed her at first: she'd quietly slipped behind him. When she squeezed his arm, he turned and scowled, wondering why she touched him like that – so openly, for all to see.

She whispered that they should leave; she wanted to speak with him. Then she turned to the class and thanked them for coming.

"Thank you, Tanya," they chanted flatly, as they did every day.

"And thank you, Dr. Pluss," added Dora.

"Thank you, Dr. Pluss," the others echoed.

As they entered the corridor, Pluss spotted Director Moorman lingering nearby. A petite woman with shortly cropped hair and an unkempt appearance, she often seemed to radiate something savage. As their eyes met, he was confounded by her angry glare. Her gaze resembled that of a vicious animal but one that was also nervous and vulnerable, behaving as if it was cornered and desperate.

Expressionless, even proud of his carefully controlled *flat affect*, he continued toward her. But as he approached, she turned and darted away.

* * *

Pluss shielded his eyes from the sunlight as they crossed a courtyard and walked toward a scrawny tree planted at the far end. Beneath a sparsely leaved bough, a metal table was cemented into the floor, its legs spotted with rust.

Tanya scattered her papers across the grimy table, hoping to create the appearance of an official meeting. Then she asked why, during the lecture, he'd seemed to grow entranced.

When he refused to answer, she shifted the conversation to the subject of the director. Lately, Moorman had been asking some rather odd questions. Perhaps she suspected that they were having an affair. Moorman was even inquiring about the doctor's methods and professional demeanor.

Although Tanya was confident that none of the staff would betray him, she remained concerned. Moorman had also questioned several of his patients. Certainly, they couldn't be relied on. For one thing, they were too naive to be prudent. For another, they could easily be encouraged to say something that she might later use against him. And some of Pluss's remarks, especially if taken out of context, would prove to be damaging, to say the least.

Pluss listened patiently, but when Tanya finished he assured her that there was no cause for alarm. Ultimately, Moorman was powerless. Perhaps a petty annoyance, but nothing to fear. Yet Tanya grew insistent. Recently, Tanya had observed Moorman questioning one of his favorite patients: Jonah Israel. Ordinarily, Moorman would avoid direct contact with a patient. It was believed that she feared them – or was even disgusted by them.

Tanya suspected that she would only be interrogating Jonah so persistently in order to build a case against Pluss.

He tried to assuage her concerns, but he added that it wasn't the right time to discuss it.

At this, Tanya lost her patience and angrily bolted away.

Alone again, Pluss marveled over her apprehension. She'd even wondered if he'd been *mesmerized* during his lecture. And it was true; he was a bit carried away by that superb etching. Indeed, it was alarming how the world of the beaux arts continued to instill such passion.

Relaxing his mind, Pluss allowed his imagination to drift. He envisioned the portrait dissolving further, into a Cubist rendition, until it finally transformed into his own worn, haggard face: a self-portrait, with lines of fracture. He imagined a slender quill, freshly pared at the nib and dipped in lustrous ink, its path a scratchy drawing-forth.

Then he recalled his old painting studio, with its floors splashed in rainbow hues. It was as if an olfactory hallucination was tickling his nostrils and triggering memories of those lost hours: mutely entranced before a shimmer of color, wet and pure. A primal density, bearing an import and meaning all its own. No existential shadows there; no hallucinated woes; no badly timed messages from the unconscious; no endless psycho-sessions; no talking cure. Only a pure reign of light and form. A liberal dripping of paint. A woody odor of varnish. A spotless canvas, afloat upon a bespattered wall. The pallid surface awaiting a touch: a fateful choice of cinnabar or cerulean. A tightly stretched horizon of permeable gesso absorbing a final tincture of incarnation.

Thus, a cosmos: bright, sinful, and wonderfully imperfect.

But he'd renounced it all: perhaps, without proper consideration. He'd hoped – naively, it seemed – to forge beyond this swarthy image of the soul and into the very analysis of it. But what had he really accomplished? Why retire from such fruitful hours to instead immerse himself in dire tomes of medical prose, with their placating gurgle of "sanity" and silly drivel of healthy hocus-pocus? Now, he wondered if something essential had been forfeited, made irretrievable.

Certainly, in life there were errors that resulted in irreversible conditions. He, of all people, knew this to be true. And he wondered if this had been one of them.

* * *

Pluss coughed his way through billows of cigarette smoke that whirled lazily around the room. Wall-length mirrors glared under flickering florescent lights. Battered chairs and worn-out sofas, gutted of stuffing and redolent with mold, were scattered about. Several skinny old men and women sat round a grimy table, sipping their drinks.

Stuart Myzer was reclining on a rude wooden bench, his coffee cup steaming beside him. He was so detached, so uninspired by life that Pluss had come to admire the purity of his laziness and sloth. Besides eating and sleeping, his only remaining passion was to unmercifully tease the other patients who wandered about the asylum.

Stuart was especially fond of annoying Angelica Pinn, who was often seen pushing a cart from which she dispensed used clothing and other tattered donations. Angelica was also prone to preach: a quality that deeply disturbed Stuart. Sermonizing, he complained, was an unbecoming form of behavior, especially for a fellow mental patient. He couldn't comprehend why it was tolerated. After all, he reasoned, why bother getting committed if you can't enjoy some peace and tranquility while relishing your free cup of morning coffee?

One day, as Dr. Pluss listened to Stuart elaborate on the relationship between eternal peace and caffeine, Angelica burst into the room.

"I have faith in God! *Faith!* That's what I have."

"Faith in God, Angelica?" Stuart assumed a soft, gentle tone as she regarded him disdainfully.

"Yes, Stuart, I do."

"Then why did he make you mentally ill?"

Stuart's booming laughter pealed across the room as Angelica, now pouting and mumbling, pushed her cart in widening circles until finally slipping away.

Pluss questioned Stuart and several other patients, but no one had seen Carlos Urebos. He decided to recheck Carlos's room but then discovered that the elevator was stalled.

While awaiting its descent, he observed the patients queuing at a nearby dispensary. When a nurse cranked up a metal shutter and began to distribute medication, he was overcome with a sense of déjà vu. He concentrated on her mechanical movement: her fingers nimbly selecting tablets, then counting out the doses and administering them. Absorbed by her hypnotic gesture, Pluss suddenly recalled a dream:

He'd awoken that morning from an extraordinary scene: a group of patients seated round an elegant dinner table, with a brightly colored pill placed upon each porcelain plate. After swallowing the tablets, they each commented, with great cheer, on the "cuisine":

"Delicious Prolixen," said one. "Marvelous Navane!" exclaimed another. "And the Thorazine, so well done …" "And have you tried the Stelazine? Quite a treat!" Indeed, it was a Mad Hatter's party of psychotropic delight!

Emerging from his reverie, he again pressed the elevator button and cursed at its delay. Then he remembered the letter. Unfolding a scrap of paper, he studied an uneven scrawl:

DO NOT FOLLOW
JEHOVAH WITNESSES

It's nothing to masturbate. In Puerto Rico, where I was sent to mate a "she" pig with a "he" pig, I used to watch them, and my penis had an erection. Instead of attacking the pig, I'd masturbate. This saved me when, one night in the park, I saw a pair of teens kissing and hugging. Instead of attacking the girl, I masturbated. The only reason the Bible forbids it is to warn us not to do it in public. Women do it too. But don't kill me. You'll get nothing by that.

C.U.

Pluss crumpled the note as the elevator opened. A pungent odor of unwashed bodies drifted from the densely packed compartment. He squeezed in, wedged between the silent passengers, and waited. But it refused to budge. Others boarded, pushing him farther back, until the doors creaked to a close. As it rose with an ominous lunge, he amused himself with the thought of Sister Evelyn – who had handed him the note earlier that morning – reading and rereading Carlos's distinctly pagan proclamations.

As far as Pluss was concerned, Carlos exemplified the type of independent, solitary patient who was better off left alone. When in need, they would announce it in their own unique, idiosyncratic manner. But until then, they would drift through their respective, isolate worlds, following a path of indecipherable, impenetrable logic. Which was another way of saying that he knew very little about Carlos except for the creation of his allegorical pig, his proclivity to cite biblical verse, and his therapeutic philosophy of liberated self-love.

Carlos's room was arranged in a sparse fashion. Other than a cot, an end table, and a folding chair, it was so devoid of possessions that it seemed austere rather than merely impoverished. Somberly painted religious icons, which hung on a wall beside the bed, highlighted this cloistral atmosphere. As Pluss studied the images, he felt Carlos's gaze following his every move.

In his late fifties, Carlos appeared to be much younger. With his lean, muscular frame and ruggedly handsome features he resembled an attractive yet battered pugilist. And he was also known to wield a dangerous physical force. His dossier warned that it didn't take much to trigger his temper. Regarding Carlos carefully now, Pluss was startled by his paranoid expression.

Carlos shifted restlessly in his chair until finally blurting out: "I know what you're thinking, doctor. I don't go to church because God isn't helping me. And because the problem I have is due to religion. In Puerto Rico, the ones who were going to kill me were Catholic. I don't know why I was so mistreated. For seven years, I was locked in Manhattan State Psychiatric Hospital. Now, I have neither friends nor relatives. *Nothing*."

"Any dreams, Carlos? Sometimes they hold the key, you know."

Staring menacingly at Pluss, Carlos stood up and slowly approached. But he continued past him, stopping at a sink in the next room. Gazing at his reflection in a mirrored medicine cabinet, he grimaced as if disgusted and spat into the basin. Then he returned to the edge of his neatly made bed. Pluss leaned back in a creaking metal chair, trying to appear relaxed.

"Dreams, doctor? When you're sick from nervous illness, you get *nightmares* … with your mother. She stands above, points a gun, and says: 'Do this, now! Or else: *Boom. Boom. Boom.*'"

Lately, several of his patients had been besieged by explicit Oedipal dreams. Although it was easy to discount Freud's literal interpretation, Pluss felt that, at the very least, they were bad news, signifying the eclipse of a fragile ego by the overwhelming force of the great mother, *psyche*.

"I'll tell you why I'm so troubled, doctor. People from my own family mugged me. Cursed me. Told a pack of lies. My ex-wife kept me awake at night, playing card games. They tried to make me sick! My own mother said nasty things. She wasn't supposed to do that. And you know my sore-throat problem? Well, she said I was making noise like a *pig*. That I wasn't sick but was *hot,* for a woman! But I forgive her …"

Carlos returned to the mirror and reexamined himself. It was as if, in studying his reflection, he could no longer find any trace of himself – as if all that remained were the glimmers of a spirit that had now come to possess him.

Following another coughing fit, a streak of color returned to his livid face. "Thank God, nature gives me some relief. Now, I don't have so much phlegm to spit. Yes, my sore-throat problem has improved. Still, I hate my mother. They say that a man should be at peace with his mama, but I don't think so."

"Carlos," Pluss sighed, "some are just *bad* mothers. And remember what Jesus said: 'If any man comes to me and hates not his father and mother, and wife and children, and brethren and sisters, yea, and his own life also, he cannot be my disciple.' That's why he also said, 'I come not to bring peace but a sword.'"

"Doctor, I never want to see my family again."

"And didn't he say …" Pluss furrowed his brow as if attempting to recall the exact verse from the Apocrypha: "'A man's foes shall be they of his own household'?"

"Maybe he did say that, doctor." Now Carlos creased his forehead as if he, too, was hoping to recall the Savior's precise thoughts on the matter.

"Why, he even said, 'I've come to send a *fire* on the earth.' You see? He's speaking directly to you, Carlos."

"He is?"

"Why, yes! He's saying that your hatred is like a flame. That it's just and good. That it has *purpose*. That is, detaching from the root of your suffering, which is your mother. Even Buddha said something similar: 'Detach from the source of your torture, and leave the desire of it far behind.'"

"Amen. I'm all for that, Dr. Pluss."

"That's why Jesus says that the father shall be divided against the son, and the son against the father."

"But it's my mother that I hate most, doctor."

"Well, then, if you want to be his disciple, Christ says

that you *must* hate your mother. Then you should forget about her and become your own man. That is, if you want to be happy. And that's what Christ represents: being your own man, and finding your source of contentment. You see, he wanted to be crucified. But you, you just want to be left alone."

"That's so true. You're a smart man, Dr. Pluss. Yes, I see your point. I'll write her a letter and tell her to fuck off. Thank you. It's a fine solution. I'm feeling better already."

The glowing rays of a midday sun cast Carlos in a luminous halo. He remained seated at the edge of his cot, quietly studying his verse.

As if Carlos were posed in a *tableau vivant*, Pluss noted the principal artistic elements: the dignified air of self-discipline; the lofty presence of a noble, spiritual light; the somberly toned religious icons hanging upon the wall (the paintings within a painting!) that accented the notion of a persistent strife and struggle. All these elements worked in tandem and seemed to reflect the enduring search for inner vision.

Pluss was so taken by the portrait's Renaissance clarity – the spiritual light animate, in abundance, and vitalizing the quest – that it was only upon leaving this otherwise stark chamber that he realized he'd forgotten all about the note concerning the pig!

Now, he fancied its bristly elongated snout: a slimy pike pushing him away from the asylum and its claustrophobic grip, out to the littered pavements of Sumpfin Boulevard.

Pluss searched the street for signs of a mythic swine: a trail of its droppings, steaming and clustered, with the rank pellets cutting a swath across the asphalt jungle and leading him directly to a historic church, located on a nearby hilltop.

The quaint granite structure – complete with white wooden steeple – appeared to be an anomaly amidst the sprawling glass, steel, and concrete clutter of the surrounding urban landscape. His patient Jeremy van der Clove had claimed that it was located high on a hill because churches and creeds require some pretty elevated thinking; don't you agree, Dr. Pluss? But Pluss maintained that it was merely a forgotten site: now safely landmarked but largely ignored by the local populace. Which made it a perfect retreat. Wandering through the adjacent graveyard was a delight that he savored for moments such as this, when he needed to escape and walk unencumbered beneath the big droopy boughs of the old spruce trees.

Once, he'd even ventured into the church and discovered an unusual mural adorning the chancel walls. It was a fresco of larger-than-life-sized nudes: women bearing voluptuous breasts and rosy thighs, frolicking joyfully round a lush, verdant, Edenic landscape. He couldn't recall the theme – no doubt, some allegory from the Bible – but, whatever it was, such festive joy was as impressive as anything from Genesis, and all of it rendered in such loving detail!

He'd spent the greater part of an afternoon admiring it. Upon returning to the asylum, he'd described the peculiar vision to Tanya. But when they returned several days later, the colossal fresco was no longer there. Instead, a monotonous beige hue covered the surface of the wall. As Tanya said shortly afterward, such things were

difficult to imagine.

Pluss circled round the neglected churchyard, then sat upon a rotted bench, its uneven slats blistered with flakes of pale green paint.

Weatherworn tombstones engraved with winged moons slanted to-and-fro across the yard. His attention drifted to a tawny-colored Gothic marker bearing a sharply etched skull with oval eyes. He stared at it. The death's head reminded him of Director Moorman's anguished scowl. He'd never disguised his dislike of her, yet her unrestrained hostility on that particular day was unusual. Had her suspicions about his affair with Tanya shifted to certainty? Perhaps, as Tanya believed, she was jealous. It would account for the increasing amount of time that Moorman was allotting Tanya in supervision. It was the perfect excuse to be near her!

Pluss wedged a cluster of spruce needles beneath his shoe. He slowly mashed it. The director's most overt symptoms were her irritability, her nervousness, her rage. Even more revealing, her guilty tone and anxious stare were symptomatic of an elemental fear.

Suddenly he imagined taking Moorman away from it all: from Tanya, from the asylum, and from her weighty responsibilities. He'd lead her here, to this sobering place, where the petty questions of the day were extinguished by the awesome maw of night and death: of rot and cold, ceaseless decay. He would lay her upon the muddy grass, her limbs sprawled beneath the bluish bars of sepulchral shadows. Yes, *pierce her bitterness,* he whispered excitedly, and enliven her flesh with a manly thrust of darker delights –

of sublunary delights, my dear!

And then, even the woeful moons would peel back their worn, grainy eyelids and glimmer in cold stone happiness that life continued here, once again.

That evening, he planned to share his fancy with Tanya. But first he observed her wriggling ritual: tugging at her tight jeans, standing on one leg and frenetically pulling at the other, hopping about the bed, barely keeping her balance as she tossed aside her scanty lingerie to expose a firm, spherical bottom.

Hours later, he awoke. Now her limbs were tossed carelessly about, her dusky skin in vibrant contrast to the luminous white sheet. He wondered how he might have portrayed Tanya earlier in his life, when he was an artist. Perhaps, with a different pose.

He pushed her until she groaned and rolled over, her plump bottom quivering with her snores. An impressive presence, he noted its heavy, earthen quality. It anchored the rest of her and drew everything down to the level of its own meaty gravity: a veritable exclamation point of corporeality! When she entered a room, it drew everyone's gaze upon itself: a derrière festooned and aglitter with eyeballs. And when she departed, all were rendered eyeless and moaning.

Tanya turned, squinted, reached out, and pulled him to her soft breasts. As he closed his eyes, her scarlet lingerie, rolled into a ball in the corner, hovered in his mind's eye: a vivid Matisse red, and the final image of the day:

En vérité, un "Grand intérieur rouge!"

* * *

The following morning, shortly after he entered his office, Sister Evelyn appeared at the doorway, wheezing and short of breath. As she approached, the nun's indigo veil caught the edge of a sunbeam. The bright ray was squared by a corner of a windowpane, forming a luminous patch that flickered across her shadowy habit until finally veering off, into space. For a moment, she resembled the stately subject of a masterly Vermeer.

As she dropped with a *huff* into the cushions of an old armchair, particles of dust swirled in the light. Pluss waited for her to catch her breath, then joined in some innocuous conversation.

Staring into Evelyn's violet eyes, he wondered at her secretive regard. Did she, too, suspect his liaison with Tanya? Suspect and even envy him? Was she susceptible to an obsession over the young Greek girl? Perhaps she even imagined running her hands through Tanya's luxuriant hair or resting her heavy head upon her ample breast. Had Evelyn prayed for Tanya – or even, prayed *to* her? Had the nun beseeched her with petition and solicitation? Or had she debased herself, submissively approaching with humbleness and humility just as, in an earlier epoch, one would approach a big-breasted goddess?

A lot of questions.

Evelyn gripped the sides of the chair, flexed her arms, and rose with another *huff*. He nodded as she muttered her good-byes. It was time for her to enter the community rooms and to chat with the patients in that ethereal tone of goodwill that terrified some as much as it consoled others. In her own unwitting way, Pluss mused, Evelyn personified the dual aspects of the godhead: horror and joy; awe and fascination.

After glancing at his notes, he moved his pen spontaneously along the page. Ambiguous forms emerged. First a snake, then a swan surged forth from a shifting, chaotic jumble of lines.

The swan wiggled its glittering neck, gracefully devouring a silvery fish. The glinty-eyed serpent crept along the sand and snapped its jaws round the head of a tiny hapless creature. The shape of the victim was vague and indistinguishable. He stared at it, nonplussed. It could have been anything, or even anyone.

* * *

"No, doctor; I don't wanna do no talking. I don't wanna see nobody. I wanna be left alone. Alone! But that girl's driving me crazy. I can't take it no more! That's what started it – Bernice, and her radio. Makes me sick! I need quiet. Quiet! *That's* what I need …"

Marilyn Boubou glared with moist, red-rimmed eyes, her fist raised in anger. But her rages were nothing new. In this despairing cubicle he'd weathered many a fit and tantrum, many a sad shout and futile gesture of resign. And it always ended the same way: with Marilyn co-

cooned like a modern-day mummy, the sheets wrapped round her head, her silhouetted profile pointing up, sarcophagus-like, with her shoes poking out from under the blanket.

"The cat?"

"Yeah, doctor. Big old cat." She covered her face again with a bed sheet and continued, "It hurts my chest. Don't know what I'm gonna do with that old cat. I wish there was a medicine to drive it out of my body. It disturbs my motion, and now the brain's gone! Been torn to pieces. Trying to figure out how to get it together, but I know I'll never be well again."

An oversized feline resided in Marilyn's chest, its stiff fur scratching her vulnerable innards. With each ungainly movement, Marilyn was reminded that she was no longer the master of her fleshy abode. For when the beast groaned, Marilyn groaned. When it scowled, she raised the roof with a wily, witchy lament. And when it lay down to rest then she, too, grew unaccountably immobile, graying with a haughty leaden despair.

He was sorry to hear that it had returned, because now Marilyn would inflate like a balloon unless something could be done to destroy it. For it was tragically convenient to blame her uncontrollable obesity and fierce primal appetite upon this crazy cat of the fleshy sphinx, this lazy Egyptian feline entombed within, lost in a drifting, timeless time of metempsychosis and crocodile gods, of the loopy eye of the *ankh* – a cross with a teardrop on top – mystic symbol for who knows what.

Into the loop one entered and never again returned, adrift with the sacred crocodiles and lost in a thick bed of reeds asway in a warm, mosquito breeze, the muddy Nile lapping you along to your mother's teat which is the grand fan of the delta: lush black earth of Moses and Nefertiti and Alexander and Akhenaton, all had wet themselves in her deltoid lap – let me wash you clean with my dirty waters and raise your material soul to a vast glittering realm of *death, death, death* – great Egyptian fantasy that delivered us to Hades, where we left this paltry life of the living and gladly marched to the everlasting realm of the deceased.

And through the eye of the *ankh* they watch us now, those of us left upon this squalid earth, every last one of us orphaned and Marilyn orphaned, too, but somehow aware that she must lie there in bed, lie there and await deliverance, lie there and suffer the cat: Akhenaton's cat, or Ramses' cat, or Nefertiti's cat, or whoever owns this damned cat, *please,* get rid of it, for – she pleads with the doctor – she doesn't know why God allows her to suffer such terrific beasts.

Such monsters of reality.

"I don't think I'll ever be well ... because someone's infesting brainwaves and someone's tampering with the brain. Maybe they even removed it. From morning till midnight, there's no peace with that thing they put in my goddamned head."

That damned cat.

"Yes, that damned cat, doctor. It took bites from me. Scratched me with its claws. Or its teeth. Or whatever. The fur of that animal, it's irritating my poor stomach. Oh, that beast. It's agony. It's too hungry. It eats all my food. It consumes all my liquids. I'm living off air! I can't even rest because, at night, it stands up and it hurts my innards."

Can you imagine?

"That's about it. That's all that's wrong. What else? It's big. It's heavy. It's no ordinary cat. An ordinary cat's small. This one's immense! Like a tiger. I don't know why it wants me, because I don't want that crude beast. If I can't rid myself of it, then surely I'm gonna leave this world. Leave, by an irritation of the skin. Or by cancer. Now I know what cancer is. Cancer is *incurable*. And that cat's a cancer. It says, me-*ow*. All my life, I'm scared of cats. They stick their heads into garbage cans, sniffing and poking with drippy black noses – for food!"

Obviously, Pluss reasoned, Marilyn had projected her unmanageable hunger instinct onto the mirage of an obstinate psychic cat. But what good would such an insight bring? With Boubou, the talking cure was useless. She couldn't think with her head, because now her bosom – the ancient seat of thought and emotion – was activated as the center of cognition, and all it could do was *meow*.

Unfortunately, psychotropic medication – something

which with to dull and obliterate the hallucination – was the only solution. But Marilyn refused to take anything because mental illness is one thing, doctor, but a cat … that's an entirely different problem, one your mental medicine can't resolve.

And since Pluss was forbidden to deceive a patient, he was supposed to refer to it only as a *hallucination*. To discuss it as a *cat* – real or imaginary – was considered *feeding into a patient's delusional system*: a negative reinforcement of morbid fantasy. But he remained convinced that accepting a patient's truth, no matter how bizarre, was the only means of building a rapport and gaining access to such peculiar realities.

But perhaps there was a path beyond such morbid truths: a portal leading to more fruitful endeavors.

Imagination
abandoned by reason
produces impossible monsters;
united with her,
she is the mother
of the arts.

He smiled as he recalled those wondrous lines, penned by the old master himself, Francisco de Goya.

* * *

When he informed Marilyn that there was a new *anticat medicine*, she blanched with surprise. It was available, he said, at all the pharmacies. If she agreed to take it, he would instruct the nurse to administer it.

As they spoke, a glimmer of hope sparked in her teary eyes. At once, she agreed to try it. Now, the only remaining problem was the need to maintain secrecy.

He tried to warn Marilyn, to dissuade her from repeating anything. Director Moorman had to be placated, and kept from the truth, at least for now. But her attention had already drifted away and she withdrew to her cocoon, her head wrapped in tattered sheets.

Discretion and secrecy. For this no longer involved the mundane tasks of a psychiatrist, or even the supramundane responsibility of someone such as St. Francis and his idyllic bestial splendors. Instead, it bordered on the magic of Goya and his fanciful lithographs, the *Caprichos*: those satiric fantasies spun in a dark mirth, with such amusing titles as *The Sleep of Reason Produces Monsters*; *Dream of Inconstancy*; and *God Forgive Her*.

Although Goya's sinister cosmos hosted no vicious tomcats, there were plenty of bloated, wide-eyed owls; demented and threatening bats that stretched like an elastic horror across a bedeviled horizon; and slinking, slouching lynx that surrounded a host of supine men. And as if this wasn't enough, those poor fellows were forever haunted by dozens of hallucinated cuckoo clocks ticking and tocking a maddening cacophonous beat across the centuries, into unexpected times and places such as this one, here and now.

He glanced at his watch. Time was short; the need for discretion great. But he harbored no illusion regarding his patients' incessant desire to prattle on to all and sundry. Persuaded by innumerable counselors to share their innermost secrets, it was no wonder they complained of feeling perpetually voided. Robbed of any fecund, nourishing darkness, unmercifully poked and meticulously prodded, they were finally deprived of every deeply harbored shame and joy.

But meanwhile

the pill grew claws
and swallowed the cat.
And that was that.

* * *

Walking across the lobby, Pluss glanced at the dusty marble floor. Again, he recalled the old studio, its wooden planks flecked with drips of brilliant paint. And here, only the shine of his shoes spotting the tiles with their faint reflections.

As he continued toward the reception desk, he noted how everything appeared duller and even more lusterless than usual. Any sense of harmony or beauty strangely escaped the place. It held little potential to reflect, to give back.

He recalled a Van Gogh he'd once seen on exhibit: a view from a window in the artist's insane asylum. Now he tried to picture it with greater clarity. As he shuffled along, Van Gogh's luminous creation gradually grew more vivid and tangible than anything that presently surrounded him. With eyes wide open yet blind to his surroundings, Pluss gazed at the precious painting: a bright star pulsing in the midst of palpable darkness.

He carefully studied the nervous brushwork. You entered a rarefied, life-giving light of spring glowing along the enormous flagstones of an engulfing corridor – the path to the artist's very own Gothic asylum. The space was tunnel-like: deep and infundibular, a corkscrewing current drawing you in, rendering you immobile, passive, beholden. A brooding arch in the foreground dominates with a sullen curve, like a pensive human forehead. Farther along, the hall sinks into a melancholy penumbra, infuscated and foreboding. Throughout, there runs a death-ridden current as brackish as the Styx, absorbing vision itself into a brightly colored ennui. And that ennui was the unique trust, the ministry even, of Mr. Van Gogh.

He was pleased to have so easily envisioned this startling image. Everything accompanying the first moment he'd laid eyes upon it had remained with him: wonderfully indelible, permanently intact. An architectonic portrait that reminded him of innumerable sorry chambers that he'd visited in hospitals, asylums, nursing homes, and all such wayside, marginal spaces – all exuding an inherent hollowness, an ultimate lack of warmth or glow. You stepped into such places and your emotions were gutted: summarily defiled and trampled upon. And they had insured it so deftly, in room after room: a sweeping autumnal breeze of uniform despair.

A pithy remark by his patient Jeremy van der Clove had said it all:

A vacuum located in social space.

Now, he understood! And Vincent had carved this into paint with all the force and bravado a madman can muster – which is a considerable lot – yet that same malign vacuum, that same numbing plague of social space was still unnerving men today: still alive and well, still running rampant.

He paused, suddenly feeling blank. As his vision petered out, he felt a bit cottony between the ears ... perhaps, he thought, something akin to a *caffeine psychosis,* only in milder form.

As a child, he'd imagined his skull as a chamber inhabited by miniature men who scurried about inside. The ears were windows; the nose a furnace; the men the functionaries responsible for consciousness. Later on, as an adult, he'd imagined it was filled with substances just as fanciful: subatomic molecules bundled into diaphanous tissue stuffed neatly into the brainpan. All with which to explain that tense, nervous, excitable something that surged through his overly charged mental apparatus!

Emerging from his trance, he found himself standing beside the receptionist's desk. Embarrassed, he realized he'd been there for quite some time. Dreamily, he gazed at the squat woman seated before him.

"Well, good morning, Dr. Pluss." It was "B," his favorite receptionist, who operated a switchboard. Bemused, he continued to stare, then smiled.

Lost in thought,
aren't we, doctor?

He wondered why they called her *B*. He was curious what it stood for, but he would never ask. For he wished to retain his association of this nasally toned receptionist with the buzz of an actual *bee*. Hence, a *busy bee* or *busybody*: a human *being* whose primary function was to plug ungainly rubber cords into tiny black holes. She was the perfect personification of a helpful insect, transporting gobs of thought-pollen from one receptor to the next, passing pollen-data here and pollen-data there – and always busy, buzzing, and productive!

"*Lost in thought!* My word, B, what a coincidence! Yes! A bit lost in thought, indeed. And how are *you* feeling today?"

"Oh, fine, doctor, just fine." she grinned, then poked her stiff beehive hairdo with the rubber tip of a long yellow pencil. "Earlier this afternoon I saw Jonah Israel. He was searching all over for you, doctor. You know, he loves talking with you."

Pluss admired her natural, unaffected manner: her glibness even. Although she lacked the slightest understanding of the most basic psychological notion, B did notice the simple things. Such as how a patient dressed. Or if he was socially active. Or what his verbal tone betrayed as he approached to inquire if the mail had arrived or if anyone had called. And although they rarely received any letters, or calls, or visits, B would always encourage them with her vibrant, cheerful enthusiasm.

And just as she cared for his patients, Pluss was certain that she cared for him, too. He even considered her as a sort of comrade. While the others grew restless over her incompetence at the switchboard, he remained charming and composed. He especially enjoyed watching her plug the wires into the sockets: a spastic, octopus-like frenzy directing her every movement. Invariably, she'd connect many of the callers to the wrong rooms, thereby increasing the patients' paranoia. But he considered this to be one of the few forms of entertainment in the asylum: a place that was, at times, *unnecessarily morbid*.

While he searched for something to say, a familiar

voice greeted him from behind. He turned round to marvel at Tanya, who suddenly appeared in her vintage white dress:

Her emerald
dress an antique:
magenta rose-petal
prints jiggle and sway,
leaves stirred,
my invisible desire.

Her dress a veil,
hiding her.
I painted every fold,
every crease
a tortured longing.

Unspoken words
tremble
beneath her train.

He nodded, then they departed.

* * *

Once they were alone at the bottom of a stairwell, Tanya pointed up, then crimped her fingers into the Sign of Four. Realizing it would be useless to protest, he silently acquiesced. She'd gotten it into her head ... a rendezvous in 404 ... and that was that!

Halfway up the stairs, she paused, wrapped herself in his arms, and nuzzled against the lapels of his suit. Pluss sniffed at her lustrous hair: a woody, earthen fragrance, like a forest after rain.

Upon reaching the next floor, he peered into a corridor, then quickly inserted a key. *404*. It was fittingly dubbed, he thought: an institutional, padded-cell sound to it – so fitting for a couple of psychos such as themselves!

As the door screeched to a close, he let go a contented sigh: a propitiatory sign of thanks. Now, they were safely ensconced in cool sheltering darkness. He regarded the chamber as a secure, nurturing womb. To be sequestered there was to escape: to hover in an indistinct, nebulous nothing.

He loved the room because it was functionless and forgotten. Its lifelessness inspired him; he was incumbent to revivify, to render it animate. And he could do so only through her.

Embracing Tanya in his wiry arms, he danced her through the voluptuous darkness, spinning her round and round in a space so infecund and sterile – so reeking of futility and despair – that he was certain it bore down to its very atoms the unmistakable brand of the nameless and void.

* * *

In a moldy conference room, he quietly listened to Jonah. *God*, Jonah mumbled, *God.* But Pluss's attention gradually shifted to the dust that had coated their bodies as they moved through their secret chamber. Mere dust,

and to dust ye shall return,

yet a dust uplifting and holy, redolent with Tanya's scent. How to reconcile such extremes? On the one hand, Tanya's fruity aroma. On the other, the dry, metallic tincture of a dismal little room.

Meanwhile, Jonah continued to mumble. An extrapolation now, on the deity's various problems. The cosmogonic quandary. But Pluss ignored him. Instead, he pondered the scents: one absolute and animating; the other riddled with dead skin, flaked eyeballs, clipped toenails.

That was the mystery. But perhaps there was a thread underlying such disparate, distinct entities.

Finally, he remembered Jonah, who possessed his own strange tale. Perhaps, he thought, Jonah might know. Perhaps the unconscious could be summoned directly through him – via the immediate portal of one already hallucinated. Pluss had often wondered if the fluid accessibility of a schizophrenic psyche could be put to better use. For, at that very moment, Jonah's words might contain a clue … or even a solution.

He leaned forward, and then he began to listen.

* * *

But the wearisome talk of God had suddenly triggered a nosebleed, so Pluss offered Jonah his handkerchief. After Jonah blew his nose, he opened his mouth for a moment to reveal blackened rows of teeth.

"Sometimes I was psychic," Jonah continued, "assuming the personalities that she was preparing for me: Robert Lipshitz, Nelson O'Brien, Raymond Kaminsky." But Jonah refused to flee from the asylum or the question of *why*: "Some analyzed it. I analyzed it." And it had deeply affected him. "A complete memory of being Robert, in the first cage in Rockland State." And Freud's admonishment that the second cage housed Raymond, but then adding: "But I thought that was Nelson O'Brien!" And cureless as we all are, despite the lure of Freud's hallucinations.

After a fit of sneezing, Jonah hoarsely whispered: "I finally analyzed it, all by myself. Instead of sex, I was placed in a heat cage. By Mrs. Lipshitz, by Mrs. O'Brien, by Mrs. Kaminsky. By incessant psychoanalysis. But I'm the only one – monstrous, really – who fully analyzed the problem: 'A heart forever in a cage.' It made Freud's mouth water, because I analyzed the problem from inside my cage." And then, there was God the Woman, seated in a lush tropical space, who would one day self-destruct: swinging a scalp through a warm pool of blood.

"Endless guilt, Jonah?"

"Well," he sighed, "God the Woman sends a mess. I mean, a *message*. She's guilty about everything: guilty about the whole thing. And she knows we're suffering on damnation road.

"At first, I considered God to be a man, but then I discovered God the Woman. What had changed my mind? The voices, of course. Voices saying that God the Woman is the real God, not Mr. Kreps. I was sure that God came to me as Edward Kreps. But they said, 'No, it's God the Woman, the real God.' During my childhood, I was convinced that God was a man. I didn't think of him as an older rabbi. I assumed he was a younger man. Younger, because it goes with the United States and with the modern world, where youth is respected."

And after believing there was no God?

"Then I thought everything just happens without any

explanation. I didn't believe that anything occurred as an act of highest God. When I became psychotic, I regressed to a belief in no God. But in Pilgrim State Hospital, they educated me that there *was* a God.

"By all logic, there should be nothing: just endless space. Space between space ... sky above, space below. There's just so much physical reality; there isn't endless ground. There can't be, because no God would build forever. She wouldn't spend her time building forever. There's just so much physical reality, although how it sits in endless space, I don't know."

The same God who had conceived of Tanya had created the dust and dirt. Ruler of form and decay, she ruled the roost of the nameless, almost endless odors. Pluss recalled Klee's severed-nose portrait ... Monroe's hallucinated mildew ... Tanya's fragrant bottom, moist with a salty dew. And Marilyn's cat, with its monstrous nostrils scenting for scraps. Intangible, incommensurable, countless combinations formed by a God who looked and smelled like Carlos's pig. And who would one day put her feet down, refusing to build forever.

"Endless space … space above, space below … How did it originate? Albert Einstein's theory: 1948, 1950, around the time of the hydrogen bomb, that we had endless space. The Endless Space Theory. But you'd have to build forever to conquer endless space."

Jonah's eyes began to glaze, and for a moment he appeared to be listening to something. But then he refocused on Pluss and continued: "We're supported by magnetism, really. The planet is supported by magnetism, so it doesn't fall. I heard it on the radio, and on the television: Einstein's theory that we're supported by magnetism. But to conquer endless space … it's one of the things that God can't do." Jonah flicked his tongue over his gray lips, visibly excited by the notion, and he briefly forgot about his nosebleed. "Doesn't worry her much though, highest God. It's not one of her problems. It may have been a problem for maybe fifty hours, at most. But really, it isn't one of her problems."

Suddenly his nose began to hemorrhage. Whenever Jonah got this deep into God, Pluss mused, he bled profusely.

Tilting back Jonah's head, Pluss attempted to stanch the bleeding with the handkerchief. Undaunted, Jonah continued with his tale. With his sinuses completely blocked, his twanging intonation now reminded Pluss of B, the receptionist.

"I may be one of God's problems," Jonah nervously whispered. "God the Woman sends a message. She's guilty about the cages in Rockland State. Guilty about the heat cages; guilty about the whole thing. Guilty, and suffering from damnation. Does she want to be undamned? Well, she doesn't want to be damned forever. Perhaps she damned herself for a billion years. Just to experience it. To experience everything. But for her, it's more than an experience: it's a way of life. An occupation in the world of endless space."

Guilt and damnation … Pluss regarded it as the antithesis of creation. A dismemberment in endless darkness, instead of fecundating it with a vision. It was to follow Jonah's path: an irredeemable detour along a diabolically forked road.

With the handkerchief held firmly in place, Jonah cautiously moved along the hall. Concerned over his condition, Pluss had ordered him downstairs, to the nurse.

Standing before a cracked windowpane, Pluss studied a dusky horizon. To deal with a bleeding nose was one thing; to tangle with an endless void was something else. The latter was a fitting occupation for the gods alone. For a man, it was a trap, and a fatal one. For it was to fall prey, like Jonah, to an endless analysis.

But he also imagined a solution. From now on, he'd consider everything uttered by his patient in an aesthetic rather than a clinical manner. In this way, he would render the hidden, ghost Jonah.

* * *

As Jonah continued to mull over his misfortune, Pluss maintained elaborate notes and constructed meticulous diagrams. These formed the basis of paintings wherein the most gruesome and ethereal forms were shaped by an eerie and fulgent light.

Light, more and more light! He'd adopted the phrase as a mantra, muttering the words throughout the dismal corridor and across the lusterless lobby.

More than a mere symbol, the mysterious illumination heralded a new form of awareness. He began to revere it; to proclaim its power; to imagine himself humbled by its brilliance. Now he spent greater amounts of time secreted away, all so that this beloved frequency would find its proper place: surging from the canvas and guiding him with a sort of metaphysical pedagogy. And that was his final wish: to allow it a place to purge with a sobering, ineffable clarity.

And so, when Jonah recalled being locked away, tortured in heat cages and doomed to a million-year analysis, Pluss committed the scene to paint. After extensive planning – his sketches and diagrams piling up and paving the way – he envisaged a stunning scenario:

A medley of hues riddles Jonah's skinny frame as he's strapped to a heat cage and electrocuted, his soul roasted beyond recognition or repair. It's just as the doctors had ordered – *Well done, please!* – their sleek top hats tilted in a pleasing array of angles as they relax at their café, merrily mulling over Jonah's simmering remains.

A crowd of learned physicians spills across the foreground, cannibalizing Jonah's carcass, their metallic teeth agleam with frenetic phosphorescent undulation. They hold their heads high, proud to possess such unassailable social status: to toast and to electrify; to torture freely and unequivocally; to happily commune and gingerly digest; and to torment, at leisure, the ill and maladjusted while strolling with an unhurried gait and satiated alimentary sense.

A leisurely
gentlemanly saunter,
through the voided ashes
of amnesia.

They mark themselves with Jonah's warm ash: thumbs upraised, they trace the arcane symbol of the crucifix upon their foreheads. A climactic gesture, accompanied by a dreadful *amen.* Then they adjust their top hats and make ready to leave, the atmosphere weighted with an overbearing sense of collective self-importance.

The chief of surgery is the last to exit, and he comments on the fine cuisine: comparing the patient to a dish of skillfully prepared frog's legs. Reenacting the meal, he mimes grasping the feet and gnawing at the thighs – explaining that it resembles a medieval, upside-down crucifixion. But the voice of Jonah Israel rises from the ash to note that it's upside down because he's Jewish and, therefore, Christian in the unconscious – a crucified Jesus in reverse – whereas in the case of a Christian, who's Jewish in the unconscious, an entirely different scenario might prevail …

Following an initial series of portraits, Pluss constructed similar blueprints for each of his subsequent works. His notebooks were crammed with a confusing concoction of architectonic schemata, complete with hidden symbols and codified insertions: subliminal themes that made their presence felt in each of the final forms.

Later, upon discovering the notes and sketches that were bound in red leather portfolios, a gradual awareness of just how elaborate his planning had been was revealed to us all. These formed the backbone of his work, and they comprised a secret, skeletal philosophy that divulged a deeper pattern buried beneath the visible forms.

In various drawings and paintings, Pluss depicted the diversity of life as it was then lived in the Walt Whitman Asylum. Allegories inspired, he would later confess, by having listened patiently to Jonah's spectral discourse on endless space. Something in that unique moment had freed him: not only from the problem of Jonah but also from the endless task of healing, as well.

For he'd gradually come to realize the great measure of his patient's delusion. Indeed, it *was* the nature of the gods to build endlessly: endlessly and even pointlessly. To create, undeterred, in the face of this horrific vortex:

before that eternal rival of the limited, the fixed, the incarnate.

Worshipping an endless void was the curse of Jonah Israel and of all those who traversed an elongated corridor culminating in a vacuum in social space.

* * *

The Analysis

He quietly crept along a vacant corridor. The day before, he'd envisioned her hands: delicate fingers upturned, with her palms extended in a clear, Renaissance light. Now, instead of crumbling plaster passageways, he was surrounded by crimson tapestries and lacquered panels of cherrywood. A pink marble table, set with a silver bowl, held a sprawling display of pomegranate, luscious and ripe. A centuries-old setting, yet the maiden was modern, even garish: licking her lips like a child savoring a sweet.

Her shining ebony eyes beckoned from beneath a wild crop of thick lustrous hair. She faded in and out of reach as he waded through her afterglow with a sluggish tranquility. Incessant padding. The beckoning gloam of the passageway. A perpetual gathering of quirky stuff: data required for a final collection. The investigations rarely proved fruitless, but even if they yielded little he continued his chronicle anyway, transcribing merely from habit now, repeating a sentence over and over as if lost in the trance of a penmanship drill:

What to do with this color; it isn't quite right; but I know that I'm close, my dear. *More alizarin, doctor: a little more alizarin!* Thank you, Tanya. Now turn, please, a bit to the left, a little more to the left. And he nervously kneaded his rubber erasers and patiently sharpened his long oval leads, muttering: *This is what pencils are for; this is what men are meant to do with the wandering leaden line* as he studied the first ray of sunlight falling upon her rounded shoulders, the light shifting through the hours into a smoldering, twilight Tanya. Then he would cease all muttering, cease all rumbling, consumed by the graceful model's serene pose. Her nimble figure hovered in an unspeakable atmosphere of concentration, the oily colors waxing and waning, her diminutive form poised on rough wooden planks: naked, pale, and glorious.

A *crazy* time, he liked to say, and one dense with rumor, beginning with the belief that when he'd dipped a brush into a pot of paint in the first inspired moment there issued from his taut lips a cry: not of pain or anger or even a cry of joy, but one resembling the shrill screech of a locomotive when the coals shudder with an unbearable heat and the very atmosphere – reaching a point of unbridled pressure – seems ready to explode. But this was mere rumor. All that was known for certain was that he'd begun to paint again, and the process of unleashing his furor had also served to unleash some rather curious, excitable things within him.

And there was what we'd fondly called his *new treatment plan*, one culled from the works of the asylum's own namesake:

Unjamb the doors!
Unbolt the locks!

Announcing himself in such a manner, he would stubbornly rap upon door after door, often mumbling other things as well, such as when I heard him remark:

Once, I believed
I wanted to cure,
but now I'm cured
from wanting to cure!

Upon hearing such ravings, the patients would laugh

among themselves: not from a meanness of spirit but rather out of fondness for him, engrossed as they were by the tale of his newly resurrected passion.

And when it was discovered that Dr. Pluss wandered from door to door in search of the morbid details of our lives, when it was revealed that he wished to render our pitiful affairs upon his massive canvases – to circulate among us and gather the fragments of memory and reverie that defined our fractured, isolate selves, scribbling notes that were later transformed into image and engendered by the brush – then everyone hailed him. All yearned to confess their dreary lot: a melancholy history that many now disclosed, with touching honesty, for the very first time. And not because they sought some small measure of immortalization in his panoramas but rather because they viewed his eagerness as a force that had mysteriously transferred itself into their own eagerless lives. Because his boldness lent a boldness, because his ferocious appetite for life imbued a small parcel of hope upon those who were so utterly robbed of it.

He frequented the winding corridors with increasing regularity, and he behaved in a manner that was previously unknown to us. But many of his habits remained unchanged, such as the mouthing of those bitter quotes and antagonistic notions that seemed to ricochet about his overactive brain. As he passed us by, huddled in our scattered groups or lingering in our lonely corners, he lectured – again, to no one in particular – about his vision of Christ as a *merry prankster*. And he scoffed at the animated debates over whether the Savior had ever laughed, which he claimed had enlivened the University of Paris as far back as the thirteenth century. "It's just as Jeremy van der Clove says," he exclaimed, "for they've turned him into

Christ the Crippled Cartographer!" It was believed that Van der Clove was one of Pluss's most cherished patients, and so, by now, he'd grown fond of quoting him.

But his favorite pastime was recounting the tales of Jonah Israel, who had stolen most of his time and concern. Pluss had finally realized the unique effect that Jonah had had on catalyzing his artistic fervor, and it was to Jonah that he would often turn for inspiration.

When Jonah complained of his unfulfilled longing for love, Pluss would exclaim: "Yes, *love*, dear case managers! And around here, we're as cureless as we are loveless!" But he no longer belabored them with his interminable lectures or fits of poesy, as he muttered more to himself and less to the others.

Throughout these *carefree days*, as he called them, he appeared to be increasingly content, acting as if such mutterings and musings were in themselves sufficient amusement. But the more positive aspects of love, which had once figured so grandly, were now nearly absent from his repertoire. This led some of the more clairvoyant schizophrenics to wonder if he was preparing for an imminent departure: not only from Tanya but from the asylum itself. For it was believed that Dr. Pluss would part from her only if he fled the asylum and traveled far away: far away from us all.

* * *

"I analyzed the problem in my cage," Jonah dryly intoned, "and the analysis continued for a million years. Occasionally, I changed identities, assuming the personalities of Raymond Kaminsky, Nelson O'Brien, or Robert Lipshitz: all boyhood friends of mine. But the analysis

continued. As Raymond. As Nelson. As Robert. The analysis. The question of why I was imprisoned. A complete memory of being Robert Lipshitz in Rockland State, in the first cage on the top floor. In the second cage was Kaminsky. In the third, O'Brien.

"And Freud listened to the analysis, glued to his television. He wouldn't eat; he wouldn't sleep; he wouldn't anything. Finally, I analyzed it: sexually aroused in a heat cage. By Mrs. Lipshitz. By Mrs. Kaminsky. By Mrs. O'Brien. Jesus Christ became Robert Lipshitz, too, when he was caged, but he didn't analyze the problem. I'm the only one in those cages who really analyzed it. *It's a hospital. Why am I in a cage?* The analysis went on. *I'm a patient; this is a hospital; why am I in a cage?*"

Although he'd heard the story time and again, the doctor listened attentively, eager to ferret out some overlooked detail to add to his painted allegories of the patients' travails.

And when Jonah grew unaccountably silent, Pluss would lean across a rickety table and whisper:

And the result of the analysis?

As if approaching his favorite stretch in an ageless fable, with a mischievous grin Jonah would lick his cracked lips and reply:

"The result? Well, Goloza, the attendant, told me it was a direct radiation theory involving God the Woman. And that's how she becomes undamned."

That's how you'll become
Jonah Israel again.

"And Freud's reaction to the analysis?"

"Freud listened to the analysis for many years. He wouldn't eat; he wouldn't sleep. He'd sit with my father by the television, or maybe in his office, and he'd listen to the analysis. He didn't want to miss it – not one *bit* of it! He called it gold. *Diamonds. Gold.* He wouldn't eat. He wouldn't sleep. He wouldn't anything. He listened to the analysis for a million years, glued to his television.

"My first doctor, Leon Leiben, also listened to the analysis. He wouldn't eat; he wouldn't sleep; he wouldn't anything. Many doctors listened to the analysis with Freud. They wouldn't eat; they wouldn't sleep; they'd listen to the analysis."

And it was believed that even Dr. Pluss would have given up eating and sleeping in his search for this analytical gold, this poking and prodding and tracing a million-year survey for some fresh nuance of dementia to catalogue and sequester into the cluttered disorder of his burgeoning archive. For he was seen knocking on doors that concealed those who no longer materialized from the squalid shadows: patients who ceased to witness the phenomenon of sunlight and who were fused into a web of dust and grime that shaped the contours of their forgotten chambers. Patients who, once upon a time, had been catalogued in a case note that was afterward misplaced, thereby causing said patient to be misplaced; and, thus, doctor, when the ink on the case notes fades I, too, will fade away; and the patients vanished, and no one was aware of their loss or mourned their absence. And when the files were placed in the wrong folders, the patients switched identities; and when the notes were crumpled or discarded the patients were themselves crushed – and liberated – by death. Of the ones surviving this holocaust of forgetfulness were those with skin so pale and rid of pigmentation that the doctor had developed a special theory proposing that, in a former life, they'd belonged to an esoteric genus of albino bottom dwellers: pink pulpous androgyns unsexed by an absolute darkness and blinded when removed from that drear pitch: a bobbing, hovering school of gelatinous moonbeams with hazy albugo eyes that cut faint traces across the black waters of a perpetual night.

He quickly sketched the straggling bottom dwellers and quietly continued on: prowling, meddling, fumbling in room after room, sifting through the respectfully offered scrapbooks of woe, scanning crestfallen diaries and disconcerting chorales of despair, listening patiently as the hours drifted by and they carefully explained the scrawl made by a blunt lead pencil eighteen years ago upon a tattered mildewed calendar that someone gave me for free, doctor, the last thing anyone ever gave me. I marked the day right there, doctor, right there, the day that I was presented with this lovely gift to keep the time. And a good gift it was, too, Pluss would say, it's lasted you eighteen years, hasn't it? He calmly stood by and silently waited as they opened drawers packed with garments of misery stiffened from disuse; he scrutinized rotted bundles of ancient starched underwear and bloodstained handkerchiefs and mismatched socks of incongruous size riddled throughout with gaping holes; he ogled and ogled but found nothing. He snooped through frowzy closets and peeked with uncertain anticipation at battered hulks of dilapidated suitcases as they cheerfully accommodated him saying, doctor, I lost the key to that damned thing; could you help me pry it open? Perhaps it contains what you're looking for: a secret formula for your compositions. Yes, we've heard of them, doctor.

And he'd unzip old corroded leather pouches that crumbled with a flurry of maliferous odors. He'd unbolt stubborn tin boxes that contained crackling parchments and feeble-minded letters browned at the edges and carefully folded into tiny rectangles. He'd examine embrittled photographs from fifteen or twenty-nine or forty-four years ago, doctor, when I first arrived; but when I looked around I saw no purpose in celebrating this putrid place with my old pictures, because they were from happier days, doctor, happier days; you understand, don't you; I know that you do, doctor. And he searched and searched but hadn't the foggiest what he was looking for, prying and obtruding and disrupting, although no one seemed to mind because there's been nothing in my life to disrupt for the last fifteen, or twenty-nine, or forty-four years, doctor; extending his elongated head into the ashes of a forgotten holocaust and in this manner discovering a woman who confessed that she'd been born in a toilet bowl, doctor; my mother was sitting on a toilet when she had me. Have you ever heard of such a thing? Can you imagine? And he replied, No, I can't imagine a mother so cruel to reveal that to her daughter, but listen, dear: it doesn't matter how you come in, because we all go out the same way. What way's that, doctor, she asked, and he said quite seriously: You meet the same bums on the way down as you do on the way up, so you better be good for goodness' sake. And they both laughed, although who knows if they understood what anyone was really saying anymore. But he worried less about the problem of comprehension, often remarking in his mumbling discourse that those who chase after understanding are the most empty headed of all, just as those who speak the most of God know him least, as the old expression goes. But he'd falter when attempting to remember who had said it first, or where he'd first heard of it, because all that seemed far less important to him, having himself abandoned the need to understand, to quote, to memorize, to soliloquize, to mouth learned stretches of poesy, to recount fragments of culture, culture is here he'd say right here at the Walt Whitman Asylum.

And he'd wander with a patient trailing beside him as he explored the crannies and crevices of the musty labyrinth, poking his head into hovels redolent with deadly sweet putrefaction or littered with heaps of glass eyeballs, each bearing faint traces of once having loved, once having floated in a tincture of joy, once having strained with desire at some beautiful thing and laughed at it, once having been graced with the hues of a rainbow in a spruce moment of youth, of spring, of love is in the air, and at that moment believing in the heart, mind, and soul that all will work out, all will be well, all will fall into place in the end. But instead, over the edge of a foul dark precipice falls a heart, a mind, a soul – plummeting into dismembering collapse – and the eyes roll and cast a final glance into this bleak void.

And the fossils bear these imprints, doctor; something was terribly wrong during this Pleistocene period of the soul; this species has suffered a terrible calamity. Like paleontologists pondering the stubborn mysteries of extinction, Pluss envisioned the physicians of a future millennium poring over his patients' queer dossiers, whirling their bright inspectroscopes over the aberrant records of a type of man that those in this distant aeon could not fathom. At best, they might comprehend in mere, isolate detail, but they'd never penetrate the essential mystery of this pathetic calcification of the spirit, gentlemen. Such an age you cannot imagine – even with the abundance of your doodlebug data! To these future bards, he'd explain that, no, it wasn't a cry such as Freud's dispirited moan; not a Viennese wheeze, anal and frustrated and anemic, no; this goes far beyond such simplistic doctrines. For, if you'll have a look over here … and with his magic brush Pluss would paint Jonah as a bigger man than Freud: as a larger man, but one with thin arms and tiny fingers. And Jonah would open his clenched fist to reveal a glittering diamond, and he'd take the doctor's hand and place the colorful stone upon his cold palm, saying:

Diamonds, gold, doctor.
The analysis!

And the two could often be seen ambling along the desolate panorama of the winding corridor like a pair of old bachelors twiddling their witty tales, with Jonah trailing beside the doctor as he banged on doors and opened drawers and scanned unreadable journals and unraveled the spindizzy ravings of such a one as Jeremy van der Clove, who at once explained, Why, yes; here, doctor, here it is:

Infinity at the Point,

at the very center of the circle. The circle representing the cosmos, which is actually an atom of *Transcendental Lithium*. Yes, doctor, *Transcendental Lithium*: that's all there is to it! And look here: this ellipse is the path of the electron, which I've identified as the *Orbit of the L-Shell*, which stands for *Love*. Yes,

the Continuous Cosine Wave of Love,

and also *Lithium*, and of course the *Loot of Lima,* the three L-gods orbiting round God as *Infinity at the Point.*

That's how it all started: the real big bang theory. What do you make of it, doctor? while Pluss jotted: *L-Shell*; *Loot of Lima*; *Infinity at the Point* – PAINT IT! And Jeremy would continue: This, why, this is a drawing of a church. And I put it here, at the upper right-hand corner, because it requires some *pretty elevated thinking*; don't you agree? Yes, and it happens to be a Mormon church, and thus my equation: 26 = CW = MM = CUNT IN U.S. WAVE. *C* being the third letter of the alphabet, and *W* the twenty-third, which added together equals twenty-six, which divided in half equals thirteen; and the thirteenth letter is *M*, which, times two, equals *MM*. That is, a *Motor Migration*, as there was a *Mormon motor migration* across the country, or at least as far as Salt Lake City, following in the footsteps of Joseph Smith, and Humphrey and Brigham Young.

But you wanted to know about the CUNT IN U.S.

WAVE, didn't you, doctor? Well, I did that on account of a great deal of masturbation, up there in the Bronx. I wrote to the editor of *Screw* – a very coarse, very rough, but very *informative* newspaper – and said that these mobile and polygamous Mormons have been making a continuous wave, a *cont-in-u-ous* wave, a Cunt in U.S. Wave. Do you see? I put it in this coarse form for the editor of the *Screw* newspaper. Do you know that he claims it's the *world's greatest newspaper*, doctor? And Pluss said no, Jeremy, I didn't know that, as he jotted in his book: *MM, Mormon Motor Migration, cont-in-u-ous wave* – PAINT IT.

Pluss crammed his pockets with ambitious sketches, meandrous narrations, fragmented logs, and hurried transcripts, everything rapidly penciled as the patients rambled on, scribbling in a shorthand that even he found difficult to decipher, sometimes composing on the back of a memorandum if he was caught empty-handed as he happened to overhear something of interest while passing an open door, or disembarking from the odorous elevator, or parting the billow of smoke in the community room, drafting and sketching like mad, then stuffing it into his pockets to analyze later on: to file, index, append with diagrams, annotate with proposals, and footnote with further elaborations, everything carefully classified for a future inquiry or exploration, and all of it finding eventual inclusion in a painting or drawing in which he'd render one more spectacle in a blossoming panorama of asylum life.

And even when he didn't appear to be writing he said he was, and we believed him, because at night he scribbled along the walls of our dreams; while by day he attempted the transcription of simultaneous conversations as the patients accompanied him on these farfetched excursions into the dismal blue outposts that had long since fallen into the shadows of faith.

Such as the day that he attempted to inspire Diana, the hunchback who liked to paint schools of cadmium-red ducks. And Marilyn stood beside them at the edge of a chipped green table and said, No, doctor, I don't have no life like other people; I'm only satisfied with this life I got because I'm *sick*. But really, I'm all right; it's *them* that are throwing their sickness at me. It's *them* with their mentally ill selves. It's *them* with their mentally ill brains. That's all; there ain't much to tell. Because I don't go *nowhere,* except maybe to take a walk, because there ain't no place to go. *Nowhere*, doctor. Because in this atmosphere, you can see that they're *sick*.

Pointing above Pluss's head, Marilyn continued, See, there, doctor, *there*, you can see it. Their *sick brain waves*. And Pluss replied: If I gave you a crayon, could you draw it, Marilyn? And when she nodded he reached into his trousers and removed a thick black crayon (yes, one stolen from the art-supplies room. But so what? For they tried to steal my soul, gentlemen. That's right: my soul). And he tore a sheet from his pad, and with his greasy black crayon Marilyn drew a silhouette of a man wearing a bowler. And over the rim of the hat, gentlemen, you will note three wavy vertical lines – menacing and hovering – to which she points and says: *They* are the ones that are talking about God, doctor. Those waves, up in the air. They're transmitting it to the people.

And I looked into the patient's eyes,
and with all the empathy I could muster

I gravely nodded, as if to acknowledge her abysmal agony and affliction. But what a paltry sum to offer!

And the poor woman, all she could do was to stare at the drawing and expel a deadening sigh. Oh, *boy*; ain't no life for me. They keep throwing their sickness at me; that's what's wrong. So I'll never be nothing. *Nothing*, really. But it ain't my sick brain, it's *theirs*, thinking all the time about God.

And Pluss nodded, Yes, God is a problem, especially that damned tripartite form of the deity with his wavy gravy vertical lines, the missing fourth part falling onto the devil, onto Lucifer to take up the slack and suffer the scapegoat. When the buck stops here; right at the top, see?

Abruptly concluding her painting of a waddling duck, Diana gently placed her moist sable-haired brush between a glistening pair of coffee-cup rings and said, Yes, the brain is a transmitter: a *cylinder* implanted by bad doctors. And now it's overworking itself, and the brain's been thinking *twenty-four hours a day*, and I can't get no relief. Couldn't you do something about it, Dr. Pluss? I can't live with this cylinder yet I can't do without it, because it reminds me to do my hygiene. And without it, I'd live like a pig.

And Pluss wrote PIG, and he concocted an elementary schemata illustrating in brief the primary conflict between man and the ancient pig god. He jotted CYLINDER, and he scribbled a note regarding the catastrophic postmodern relationship between technology and the well-being of the unhygienically disposed soul. He added TRIPARTITE BRAINWAVE TRANSMISSION, and he penciled in an asterisk with a question mark – because he was uncertain as to how to proceed, but we'll figure it out later; save it for the peace and tranquility of the night – BUT PAINT IT!

As he continued jotting and musing and treading upon the dirty green carpet as if blind to our stares and deaf to our murmurings, it was sometimes remarked that Dr. Pluss listened to his own set of transmissions: that he was cognizant of the echoes of a discourse that resounded from weeks or months or even years ago, the monotonous rambling of a patient's lament of sordid fate now surfacing and falling to his lot. All of which led him to converse as if time hadn't lapsed; as if again admonishing us that

Only the unsteady mind
breeds time,
folks,

which was once his favorite Tibetan saying. Indeed, it didn't seem to matter whether someone such as Jonah was actually there or was present merely *in voce* and was reiterating:

Why is it, doctor,
that I didn't hear any voices
in my youth?

Then I became older, and I heard voices. And on that day,

I became schizophrenic. And I spoke to a nun, who sent me to a priest, but the priest sent me to a social worker, and here I am.

Yes, here in hell, Dr. Pluss would muse aloud, here in hell. And Jonah would reply, Yes, in hell because I can't find a job, a wife, or a hobby. Because neurosis is preventing me from working, and from finding a hobby, and from finding a wife.

And then Pluss sketched the outlines of another grand painting: *Jonah versus neurosis,* with Jonah scouring the entire neighborhood for a remnant of the tripartite unity. But instead, he's led astray by church and state, signified respectively by a Tweedledee and a Tweedledum who jabberwocky a path where the healthy ones come, picking the forest clean of sickly trees and stoking a furnace with the dried-up timber of the stragglers and deadbeats.

Such is their success that they're promoted to sign painters, and they paint in red block letters: *ASYLUM ASYLUM* send us your sick and we give them asylum. But Jonah interrupts to quote Jesus Christ himself who, rumor has it, said: Blessed are the meek, for you'll inherit the earth,

and a Merry Merry Christmas
to you all.

It was believed that Pluss was so inspired by the *Merry Christmas* painting that he began the next thirty-three Jonah panels that were later discovered and analyzed *ad nauseam*. Indeed, it was the *Merry Christmas* portrait that led to his break from the asylum and his decision to spend his last days in America concluding the Jonah series, starting with Jonah being cured of paranoia at the Bulova Watch Repair School and leaving behind his persecution complex in the grim milieu of the Bulova assembly line, with its enormous clocks ticking and tocking in a nerve-wracking medley over a blood-red banner that read:

ONLY THE UNSTEADY MIND
BREEDS TIME, FOLKS

In panel fifteen Pluss portrays Jonah seated at home and – under the questionable guidance of Dr. Leiben – reading Freud's *Introduction to Psychoanalysis* and suffering a psychotic relapse. Panel nineteen illustrates Jonah's initial period of work with Leiben, with Jonah expounding on the relationship between thin-arm disease and the fear of having an inferior sexual constitution. How this causes unending distress. How the three-year-old personality constantly interrupts big Jonah and renders him unable to make conversation until a transference is established.

"The transference," Jonah adds, "is a relationship formed between a patient and a doctor; and I can't make conversation until a transference is established, but then I make plenty of conversation."

Leiben is pleased. He encourages his patient to read more Freud, to *intellectualize* his illness. But the voices continue to haunt. In panel twenty-two, Jonah wonders: "Doctor, what do you think is the cause of the voices? Is it the clamorous symptoms of *dementia praecox?* The desire to be superior? Perhaps, subconsciously I want to be president of the United States, but I don't want it *con-*

sciously. I just want to be one of the little neighborhood characters.

"The voices are about the Christian God, but I'm Jewish. The voices are something terrible. Could it be the clamorous symptoms of schizophrenia? An inability to return to my object? *Objects*. People in whom I was interested in the past. Loretta Winicore. Jane Davis. Susan Wynner. Freud calls these *objects,* doctor. Isn't that strange?

"But the voices really aren't about me. I'm just one of the little Jewish people, made to suffer because only Aunt Tillie would accept my thin arms. I suffered a fear of rejection from the outside world, but at age twenty I became unfixed. Then I felt all right about my arms, and for the last twenty years I've been feeling all right about it. I used to know the relationship between thin-arm disease and the fixation of libido, but I don't anymore, doctor. But this didn't stop me from proposing marriage to several women – at least three or four – but they all said no, even though I proposed in a very nice way, doctor, in a very nice way.

"But I'm just one of the little Jewish people. And I wrote so to the president. I said, 'Dear Mr. President, I assure you that the Jewish race is good and superior. And the Negro race is good and superior. And the Jewish race and the Negro race suffer more than any other people. And a Jewish Negro suffers more than a Christian Negro. And perhaps there's something you can do about this.'"

Panel twenty-four depicts Jonah engulfed in the smoke of the community room, where he petitions the people: "What can the president do about it? Give the Jewish people a card. A card to get more coffee, tea, food, wine, cigarettes ... I can't think of anything else. Extra medication.

A card to get something free, from the drug store. A card to prove that I grew to national fame by becoming a patient."

A card to get everything
they need
to become undamned.

"You do believe that the president knows a little about each patient, don't you, doctor? Because if he doesn't keep track of us, who does? Who? Because my mother is gone. She used to take care of me: very good care. She gave me French toast. Meatballs. Potatoes. Corn. Green peas. Coca-Cola. Pall Mall cigarettes. When I was older, sixteen, she offered me toast, with a little cream cheese. A little honey. A little jelly. And just butter. She took care of me, but she was also evil, doctor. She said I was too ugly and too stupid to find a wife. An evil remark, just at the proper point, when I'd regress and become psychotic.

"Doctor, you won't believe it, but I did the insane. I took no sleeping medication. In my childhood, I slept naturally. An act of God, sleeping without medication. I believe that's in the field of philosophy: people without medication, just sleeping at night. What do you think? I did the insane many times. I did the insane by going to school. I did the insane by trying to move from my neighborhood. I did the insane by trying to graduate from college and make money at a job. Because my family has money, doctor. They paid for my stay at the Walt Whitman Asylum. I did the insane when I knew they had money, yet I tried to make it on my own. What should I have done instead? I should have remained at home and listened to my radio. I should have listened to my father. He said not to be *faselig.* That's German, for being mixed up. He always listened to my problems, but one thing he wouldn't do was to get me a model railroad. And that's a problem, doctor; that's a problem.

"Another problem is the voices. They say they'll make the Christian God into Elizabeth Taylor. That I'll be exterminated, yet survive: as Harry S. Truman, or Franklin Delano Roosevelt, or Robert Lipshitz. Disintegration; reintegration, so I won't really die. Just as Christ disappeared on the cross and reappeared on the planet Heaven, this is proof that life is everlasting and that there's no danger of dying. When you disintegrate, it doesn't mean you won't reappear. Because death is caused by a death drug. And a life injection, a life drug, counteracts it, and brings a person back to life, with just a life syringe."

In panels thirty through thirty-three, Pluss painted the final solution, in which Jonah reveals that a life syringe isn't a sufficient remedy: "Because of my mother's plot that I wouldn't relate to anyone but her. My father would die, then she'd marry me. That's all, doctor. But she made the psychosis of it. She made me psychotic. I wouldn't relate to anyone but her, Aunt Tillie, and my cousin Sabina. Only to women in the family. And when my father died, she would take me out of the psychosis and marry me, because she couldn't stand my relating to other women. She was in love with me, but that's not allowed. That's God's law. It's not permitted.

"She was mostly a good person, my mother. Sweet. But I didn't care for this plot. Why become psychotic? Better to be like my father, who was a genius at business. What did he do? He was a grocer. But I'm not jealous of him. I've come to a peaceful medium about my father. I didn't kill him. The Oedipus complex, I'm not. I have nothing to do with it. I refuse to become the Oedipus complex. It would make me feel inferior, actually killing a father and taking a mother. Instead, I want to feel superior. I didn't want to marry her. I wanted to marry Susan Wynner or Rosalyn Chayer.

"Susan and Rosalyn. There was a split. One was serious: a depressed type. That was Susan. Evil, maybe. But Rosalyn was a good person. Mad, frivolous – up there, up. Mostly, I'd gravitate toward Rosalyn. Because I didn't want to marry my mother. And, after all, who wants to become psychotic?"

With the tip of his fine, No. 2 brush, Pluss wrote NO ONE in a shaky luminous scrawl.

* * *

"Careful. Nothing but ashes here. Ashes ten-to-twelve-feet deep." The guardian of the crematorium spoke kindly, keeper of former heat cages now turned to dust.

He escorted Pluss around the factory. Here, the voices remained silent: mere names, carved into cold stone walls. Still, a number of questions remained:

Had Director Moorman placed a tail on each of his patients? Did she monitor their days and relentlessly record their dreams at night?

What was her reaction upon hearing of the mysterious

cat cure? And why had Marilyn been spared any retribution? Would removing her have raised too many eyebrows? Or were there additional factors that were now impossible to trace?

Had Sister Evelyn stepped into the ray of sunlight to trigger an aesthetic reaction in Pluss? Much as Tanya might flirt to excite him or the director might scowl?

Did Tanya escort anyone else to room 404? Why were so many of her associates catapulted into such abject self-abuse? Was it simply a case of polymorphous arousal? Or was it triggered by her overpowering, ambrosial fragrance? Would the mechanics of the stunning, alluring tincture always remain within her grasp? O would she eventually lose control of it as she matured?

And what about the eponym of the asylum? Would Walt have found solace in lending his divine name to such a sorry venue, or would it diminish his otherwise indomitable spirit? Would his jaunts through the bloody battlegrounds have instilled a proper temerity? Or was this something that even Old Graybeard himself could not have banked on?

Creeping thence steadily
up to my ears
and laving me softly all over,

he had written,

Death, death, death, death, death.

* * *

Pluss bid farewell to Agent Drain, faithful guardian and keeper of the crematorium, and he traveled backward, arriving at the coast in the evening. He followed a windy seaside path, occasionally pausing to lean over a guardrail to watch the surf crash and spill across the craggy boulders below.

* * *

Jonah stood there quietly observing the entombment. As Pluss lay in a stone sarcophagus he appeared to gaze up at the brilliant sky. Perhaps the doctor wanted one last look at this luminous vault of heaven before sliding into absolute darkness. If only the attendants would agree to pause before he disappeared into the dank gray niche. One last, ultimate meditation under that glorious spectral lid! To sink irrevocably into such a deep black pitch ... one was never adequately prepared. Surely, it was one of the final traumas of the newly dead.

And now
he is passing
through the darkness.

* * *

As the sarcophagus slid into a recess in the wall, the receptionist curtly handed a postcard to Jonah. She neither smiled nor deigned to look at him directly. In fact, she rarely displayed any emotion. At most, she seemed to regard the patients as an unspeakably filthy lot. So unlike B, Jonah thought. B, with her warm, generous, uplifting smile. Now he wondered if he'd ever be permitted to see her again.

He shuffled across the verandah and sat at his favorite formica table in the corner. From there, he commanded an unobstructed view of a sedate tree-lined street.

Everything was more orderly and more carefully attended to here. But regardless of all that, he would have preferred to remain at the Whitman Asylum. The patients here were older and closer to death. Many were confined to wheelchairs. Most were unable to care for themselves. Even the smallest of decisions were made for them. Everything proceeded according to schedule, appointment, and faithfully followed regulation.

He couldn't put his finger on it, couldn't say precisely what was missing, but it had something to do with the moments he'd shared over the years with his fellow patients. Although he'd never found a girlfriend or a wife, at least he hadn't been as lonesome as he was now. Even the additional coffee and cigarettes that he received didn't seem to help.

And then there was the troubling disappearance of Dr. Pluss. Things seemed to have gone downhill from there. Pluss had provided that extra push. He'd offered hope. Hope, from a competent authority. From an expert on psychoanalysis. Pluss would listen and advise, and afterward he left one feeling less inferior. He'd even helped to reduce the grueling intensity of the unrelenting voices.

Jonah carefully studied the patients seated round the room. Some were completely bald; others possessed ghostly strands of sleek white hair. Many were hunched over or asleep in glittering chrome wheelchairs. Such a despairing place! Surely, he was *out of place* here. There must have been a mistake. Maybe they thought he was senile instead of mentally ill. Because everyone just seemed *old*. Worn out. But not crazy. Not deranged. Just tired. Falling apart. Asleep.

With his back to the other patients, Jonah clenched the postcard and smiled a wicked, toothy grin. But this! This was certainly a red-letter day. *A red letter*. That was an idiomatic expression. It meant something special. In his *Hamlet* class, Pluss had instructed Jonah about such phrases. "To be or not to be." That was also an idiomatic expression. Or: "Long live the King!" That was another. Pluss had asked the patients what other lines from *Hamlet* were now considered as idiomatic. Eagerly scanning his book, Jonah had replied:

"I understand you not,
My Lord."

That was one, wasn't it? And, "I am dead, Horatio. Wretched queen, *adieu.*" Wasn't that another? "Thank you, Jonah," Pluss had smiled. "Thank you very much." Yes, he'd done well for himself on that particular day.

A red letter. Like a *red herring*. Another common expression, but he wasn't sure what it meant. Perhaps, a trick or a plot. To be stuck here, left high and dry like a red herring. But in any case it was a red-letter day, that much was certain.

The card was unsigned, and the smudged postmark was indecipherable. Yet he knew it was from Pluss. The doctor had finally contacted him. But he hadn't signed it, because he'd wanted the origin of the missive to remain a secret. Their secret.

Wanted to keep it a secret.

That was another colloquial expression.

The card illustrated Leonardo's painting of the Virgin, Saint Anne, and the infant Jesus. Jonah recognized it at once. And Pluss knew that he would. This was also their secret. Or at least, part of it. Pluss was well aware that he'd read Freud's essay on Leonardo. Jonah had often discussed it with him: about how Saint Anne resembled his very own Saint Sandra. Or rather, *Aunt* Sandra. And about how Uncle Moses had forced Jonah to have sexual intercourse with her, around bar mitzvah time. Even Pluss had seemed surprised. She grabbed me, doctor; she threw me on the bed. I didn't know what was happening. In Europe, it's an old Jewish custom for a boy to sleep with his aunt. What happened? Nothing. Nothing much. It's a custom from old Russia, or from Germany, to masturbate to his aunt's foot and to have sexual relations with his aunt. You never heard of it? Well, it's not known in the U.S., where it's against the law. What happened? Mostly, I lost consciousness. I didn't know what I was doing.

Jonah squeezed a lump of tobacco from his pouch, rolled a cigarette, then carefully studied the card. Baby

Jesus, surrounded by massive, fleshy women dressed in sinister robes, which were shaded with fanciful creases and folds. Shapes that Freud believed formed a subliminal contour of a bird. With a phallic tail feather, which pointed at the infant's sacred mouth.

Jonah wondered what had happened to Freud when he was a boy. What dreadful things had he suffered, to cause such fancy?

Then he fondly recalled Pluss's reaction: additional evidence, he had grumbled, of Freud's latent, ever-budding psychosis. To see birds when there weren't any. Like your classic pink elephants. (What had he meant by that?) In a baby Leonardo's mouth. Or on a Christ-child's lips.

And Freud's cigar. A phallic symbol ever present, no matter what the occasion. Cigars are phallic symbols, Freud had said, but they're also just cigars. And this, no doubt, was just a robe. Nothing more. No hidden bird. No phallic tail feather. Just a Freud, seeing things. Hallucinations. His way of life.

* * *

Tanya awoke with a start, then sighed with relief once she realized that it was only a dream.

She'd been walking along a desolate windswept Parisian street, following a man in a dark cashmere coat. The coattails flapped in the wind like a pair of birds, fluttering under dimly glowing street lamps. She could barely keep up with his rapid gait, but she managed to maintain a discreet distance behind him.

Turning sharply to his right, he slipped under a smog-stained archway. Marble statues rose on either side of the entrance, the looming figures writhing in combat. After he entered a corridor, he disappeared into the shadows.

The path opened into a courtyard hosting a glass pyramid, which was bathed in bright magenta light. Tanya paused to study the magnificent structure, then recognized it as the centerpiece of the Louvre. Overcome by the majesty of its form, she momentarily forgot about the man. By now, she'd surely lost him!

Dashing round the courtyard, she found it abandoned, the fountains' steady spray the only discernible sound. As she boarded an escalator inside the pyramid and descended toward the museum, she scanned the lobby below. Guardians listlessly shuffled back and forth, and the cavernous space was nearly empty.

She meandered about until noticing a man in one of the souvenir stores. As she approached, he stood with his back to her, stooped before a rack of postcards. He cupped something in his hand: a small object, possibly a card, which he was scrutinizing with intense concentration.

After entering the store she moved out of sight, darting behind a display rack. Cards were stacked all around: reproductions of the great works of art through the ages. Yet most depicted pieces that were completely unknown to her. She wondered if the peculiar collection was of some special import to him. Perhaps he, too, was surprised to behold this esoteric assortment of images and was now engaged in the study of one such uncanny reproduction.

She peered around the rack, hoping to obtain a better view, and was suddenly confounded. It was Pluss, his unmistakable brow looming over a diminutive card, which he clasped tenderly in his long, spindly fingers.

Before Tanya could speak, a woman approached him

from behind. Her radiant eyes were framed by a cascade of raven-black hair. There was a familiar rapport between them. Tanya moved forward, hoping to eavesdrop, but their conversation remained barely audible. Instead, they seemed to communicate in some other mysterious fashion. A mere gaze between them, and everything was understood.

Tanya knew exactly how Pluss would regard the stranger. For she embodied his feminine ideal: a bountifully endowed early-nineteenth-century odalisque, perhaps of the Ingres school, and with a wily pubescent streak of *sensual indolence*. What was unbearable (it rankled her to no end!) was that the girl bore more than a passing resemblance to Tanya herself. No mere double, she was an amalgam of all that conspired to create in Tanya a fusion of overpowering feminine essence. Like staring into a mirror, she thought, only to see the completely realized ideal upon which one was mortally, and thus imperfectly, shaped. And she didn't like it – *not one bit!* No, at that moment of sharp, prickling revelation, she felt only the dull brunt of a deft, cleverly crafted *meanness*.

* * *

At first, Jonah was pleased. At last, someone to speak with!

The young doctor sported closely cropped blond hair and steel-rimmed glasses. His manner was formal and detached. He sat rigidly, on the edge of a chair, his attention fixed upon a pad of scribbled notes.

He began the session by rapidly firing a series of questions at Jonah. Although he tried his best to answer, Jonah remained uncertain about whether the doctor approved of his replies. Or if he was even interested in what he had to say. Nevertheless, he answered as accurately and as comprehensively as possible. But the young man merely continued to scribble, all the while avoiding eye contact. There were long unnerving silences, then other questions. Questions that seemed completely unrelated to the previous ones. And then, more scribbling. And then, silence.

Jonah studied the psychiatrist as he adjusted his glasses and silently scanned through his paperwork. Perhaps, he thought, he should take the initiative. Instead of just answering questions, Jonah would introduce a fresh element into their endeavor. Something the doctor might find of interest, psychoanalytically speaking. Yes, he thought, he should at least make an effort. Because, so far, there was no transference – not even the *hint* of a transference. And without that, you had nothing. It was difficult for him to make conversation before the transference was established, but, once it was established, then he made plenty of conversation.

Doctor, I believe Tanya
is the whole problem.

Startled, the psychiatrist regarded Jonah with an enigmatic stare. For a moment, he seemed to forget about his notes.

"She thinks that I'm not her type. She's already married, but really, she wants to marry me. And this may cause a split. Yes, doctor, there lies the whole problem. Behind that brain, an insanity. Behind that clever smile, a schizophrenia … A split personality. She's not *conscious-ly* insane. But in the unconscious, or, rather, in the *subconscious* ..."

The doctor gazed at Jonah with an inquisitive expression. Perhaps, Jonah thought, it was working. He slowly began to relax, certain they were finally getting somewhere. Breathing deeply, he continued:

"Tanya tried to make me propose marriage. But of course, on the other side of the personality, she doesn't want me to propose marriage. The other side of personality: that's the problem. Freud knew that, and he had problems, too. But fortunately, I established a transference with her. Yes, I think there's a relationship there. At least, some kind of relationship. I know she doesn't want to harm me. But surely, she causes the whole trouble. Cleverly, doctor, *cleverly* she turns on the voices. Fear of life ... fear of *death*, I mean. 'Fear of life' was a Freudian slip. Really, it's a fear of death. Because, for most of my life, I would've welcomed extermination.

"You mustn't forget the unique circumstances of my birth. I was born on August third, 1935. Four years later, Panzer divisions advanced on Poland, to punish the Polish people for being good to the Jews. But my mother, who was God the Woman, used to make Shabbos. She'd bless the candles, and all that. And the insane German soldiers would see it in their visions – God the Woman making Shabbos – and they'd treat the Jewish people well, because they feared God the Woman. When they saw the schizophrenic baby, they were going to destroy it, destroy the body. But God the Woman wouldn't let them."

Pleased to have engaged in such lengthy conversation, Jonah grinned a toothy grin, then added, "I go to church now, where they give me something to make me a better person and not suicidal: the blood and flesh of Christ. He committed suicide so that we wouldn't have to. In other words, he died for our sins."

The doctor studied Jonah carefully. Even with all his topsy-turvy analytical jargon, this patient clearly lacked insight. His judgment was severely impaired. His skills of daily living were minimal. His physical appearance was a disgrace. A chronic schizophrenic, through and through. There was only one solution. He'd increase the medication, then administer electroshock. He jotted a note to schedule the ECT, then quickly excused the patient from the room.

After Jonah departed, the doctor slid his pen along the list. Whom to call upon next?

* * *

When Jonah objected to the prospect of shock treatment, the social worker smiled, tilted her head coquettishly, and addressed him in a singsong fashion: one appropriate for a child, he thought, but not for a grown man. And certainly not for someone twice her age. As she prattled on, Jonah noticed a resemblance to his old friend, Susan Wynner. It was a similarity that disturbed him, and he grew frightened. A depressive type, Susan was enshrouded in sorrow within; yet outwardly she appeared bubbly, effervescent, even superficially joyous.

"You should keep an open mind, Jonah. Learn to be more *open-minded* about shock treatment!" When he remained silent, she attempted to charm and cajole. She crossed her legs so that her short black skirt flapped open and closed – concealing, revealing –

Now you see me;
now you don't!

And when that didn't work, she gently touched and affectionately squeezed his forearm for a brief lingering moment, all the while drilling her pointed, gimlet eyes imploringly into his tattered soul.

Jonah didn't comprehend what the fuss was all about, and he remained adamant. But as he continued to resist, she began to threaten in a sweet yet sinister tone, which grew closer in pitch to the haunting refrain of Susan Wynner's shrill, eviscerating lament. Until it finally came to resemble the baleful, cacophonous voices.

Jonah screwed up his courage and gazed boldly into the heavy-lidded gloom of her bottomless stare. Then he grew even more frightened. What would happen if he didn't agree? There was something unmanning in the dire pitch of her imprisoning eyes, he thought:

A prelude to the insane state.

Yet, he tried to hold on. To remain calm. Even while the voices of extermination welled up, cresting into a booming, incessant roar, till a brimming fear of losing control overcame him. Then he realized that he had no choice but to succumb. As the voices gripped him, he nodded, "Yes, all right." And her eyes sparkled, *so joyous!*

as if all the seemingly fruitless hemming and hawing with her little boy had finally resulted in him trusting her and in accepting this glistening lollipop: her *shock.*

She was so enamored by her own suggestive powers that she leaned forward and crackled a kiss in the air, just inches before him.

* * *

They wheeled Jonah along the corridor as he mumbled to no one in particular:

A constant voice, informing me that I'm only three feet tall. Two feet, five inches, to be exact. The voices are from the people, claiming that I'm in miniature, about as big as a child. When I don't hear the voices, they do: the patients. But hearing the voices can be a pleasure. Why? Well, why not? Anything can be a pleasure. But it's not. It's not a pleasure, and I'm not a hopeless case. I flowed into the paranoid state, and I flowed out of it again.

The gurney rounded a corner as he breathed a shallow, raspy breath ... now careful to whisper only to himself ... fearful of the effect that such disagreeable expressions might have upon the guardians:

'They're making him,' the voices say, 'the Christian God.' Yes, I'm very psychotic. I may be in the insane state. If there's anything you can do. Perhaps, some medication to counteract it. Or maybe something else. I tried to do volunteer work at Goodwill Industries: the

place for the mentally ill. But Goodwill made me drift into psychosis

because Goodwill
resembles an extermination center.

I still want to be exterminated, but now it's in the unconscious. Consciously, I'm afraid of it, but unconsciously I'd welcome any means to be exterminated. In my old age, I'm becoming desperate. Perhaps if I slash a wrist, they may acquiesce. Exterminate me, instead of sending me to a hospital.

And why was extermination said to be in a man's best interest? Why such an integral part of his character … of his essential nature? He used to know the answer, but he could no longer recall.

My father's family was exterminated by Germans in a forest near their home. I believe Aunt Tillie may take me to Germany to be exterminated. One of my delusions. I'm in a delusion with this paranoia. A constant worry about Aunt Sabina, who's paralyzed in New Jersey. Do you think someone will exterminate her? I may be able to help her if I'm made into Franklin Delano Roosevelt. On the other hand, that would be bad for the people. A regression to the Second World War. The calendar would regress to 1939, and it would be the extermination of the Jews all over again.

In 1939, my father's brother, mother, and grandfather were taken to a forest in Austria and killed by Germans. My parents told me about it in 1939, 1940, when I was four, maybe five years old. I grew depressed. And it depressed my mother that my father's family was killed. My father was very tearful. He was tremendously upset that his relatives were exterminated. But it didn't bother him too much. I don't think he had depression all the time. I was sorry to hear that his relatives were exterminated in Austria. But I didn't know them; I hadn't met them.

The voices cackled along the corridor as the guardians wheeled steadily forward, now accelerating their pace.

I don't know much about my mother. She almost didn't speak to me as a child. She committed suicide. Took a pill. My aunt, my uncle, and I found her in a bathtub. This is a lot to know about her. I don't know anything else. She was a facade. She was afraid of being exterminated. I think she swallowed a pill when she was in a tub of water. Yes, she was afraid of being exterminated; this was the whole issue. More, I don't know. I don't know much about my parents. Mostly, they attended to my bodily needs. Gave me food. A television. Sent me to school. Bought me radios. Many radios.

Then she slept with me. It may have happened when I was ten. I didn't experience anything. Not a thing. She may have experienced something; I don't know. I didn't experience anything emotional, anything physical. But my father may have had a heart attack when I was ten years old. The doctor suggested a hotel to recuperate. Coronary thrombosis. He stayed two, maybe three weeks. It made my father a little against me. But nothing serious. He wasn't seriously against me.

The guardians halted and the gurney lunged forward, but Jonah was tightly strapped in, and this had occurred so many times before that he was no longer afraid of falling.

A fear of flying.

No, it was a fear of extermination. A sort of suicide. But not of flying. Flying was not one of his problems.

* * *

Of all those involved, Sister Evelyn was the one most affected by the doctor's sudden departure. On that day of malevolent influence she had remained at home, safely sheltered in the convent. A perfect day to withdraw into her chambers: spread-eagled, roseate, and flushed. An undignified constellation of circumstance in which she'd attempted to regain her composure.

And that same afternoon, all throughout the asylum, there reigned a suspicion that she'd wished to avoid a brimming of hatred and rage. To be excused, quailing and prostrate, and to fall into a profound hunchback slumber.

"Pluss has disappeared!" Tanya cried.

"In the words of the famous Dr. Lanyon," Evelyn sternly replied:

Spare me mention
of one whom I require
as dead.

As if nothing of import had occurred, Evelyn moved ever deeper into the tunneling corridor as she tended to her rounds, hobbling and wheezing from one hopeless assignment to the next. Her tortured thoughts remained veiled, forever a mystery, her motives carefully camouflaged from the other staff members. As if from a great distance, they observed her punctually completing her various tasks, each performed with an unobtrusive resolve and revealing neither passion nor disinterest.

But there were times during which Evelyn was rarely seen administering to her patients. Instead, she'd remain transfixed in some godforsaken corner, doggedly dismissing every inquiry of concern while impatiently mumbling into an ugly pool of sadness.

"In the words of Mr. Canyon, *I can bear it no more*," she would hiss at a befuddled Tanya.

"Bear what?" Tanya would inquire in meek, gentle tones, her reasoning now scarred by the disgraceful forgetfulness of a devilish self-love.

"*Foul play*," Evelyn would reply, till a pall descended over her cold violet eyes:

And the wild, infinite tale
of a professional self-destroyer.

During such alarming interludes of trembling self-scrutiny and plentiful distress, certain counselors wondered if Evelyn's dossiers contained nothing more than the unctuous farrago and worthless gimcracks of a constantly recycled narrative: a series of rehashed reports penned not as a result of actual, specific encounters between corpulent healer and tattered patient in any real, genuine space and time, but, instead, a fantasized, incorporeal discourse spun completely off the top of her head.

Perhaps, Evelyn regarded such nimble fantasies merely as white lies. Most likely, they also served a higher purpose: allowing her additional time to get on with the endlessly repetitive, none-too-pretty tasks at hand. Immersed in a falsified history of phantasmagoric rounds treaded upon pathways of despair, it was said that hers was a particularly impoverished state of mind: an absolute stasis in which the surrounding landscape of entrenched ennui was superseded by the spiraling vortex of a boundless resignation and imprisoning gloom.

* * *

"Damnation is a serious form of suffering. More than that, I can't say. Dreams? Yes, but I don't remember them. Some think that it was a dream that made me sick in the first place. Some say it was merely a dream that made me mentally ill. What do I think? Yes, it may have been a dream, about forming a sexual fixation and making it my arms that I was rejected for. And regressing to no God, to no God existing.

"There was a secret on Gerard Avenue, and it may have gone as far as Fordham Road in the Bronx, that my grandfather slept with his only daughter and produced a baby. Meaning me. But they gave the baby to Oscar and Dinah – my parents – because they were so superior. Because they wouldn't harm me, Dinah and Oscar. They wouldn't exterminate me. They wouldn't even laugh. Yes, the Jewish people may have had a secret about my grandfather. Yes, I heard voices telling me this.

"Who else knew? The visitors to the hospital. Where was the rumor spread? The rumor was spread to me. The voices say that he slept with his only daughter, God the Woman, entered her, and produced a baby. But he wouldn't keep it, so they gave it to Oscar and Dinah, for good treatment.

"There was just a voice, a message from my grandfather. He claims that he's God. It's in German: "*Ich bin Gott.*" He says that he assumed the form of all the men here in the home, and on the street, and in the subway: "*Assumed the form of many people.*"

"And now, a voice from my cousin Eddie, agreeing that my grandfather is God. And: "*Ich habe den Himmel und die Erde geschaffen.*" This means that he made the heavens and the earth. He may have done a lot of building, my grandfather. Was he an engineer? Yes, he was. What did he build? Houses, streets: that sort of thing. Tall buildings, with too many people inside.

"It's difficult to work with such voices. I even hear things about flamethrowers and acid tubs. But I don't answer them. I wonder where they originate. Transmitters on a distant planet? Perhaps they're the symptoms of wanting to feel superior, like President Wilson? And the people here, why don't they hear these voices?

"God the Woman says that it's better if I don't know about such things. When I regressed to no God, I really had a happy life. I thought that scientists had built the world, by hand and machine. Physical reality. Take from the earth. Minerals.

"The voices often speak of Christ. They say that Jesus of Nazareth, when he was caged in Rockland, in Pilgrim State cages, was made into an example. On the cross, he asked:

Father, Father,
oh why
have you done this?

You see, he also thought that God was a man.

"What do I think of rabbis? That they're evil, sadistic. Mostly, they're produced by the devil, who slept with the rabbis' mothers. The devil goes from house to house to sleep with the mothers. Who produces good rabbis? Jesus Christ. He was a Christian rabbi. Jesus and Mary, the Mother of God, slept together to produce good rabbis. Who produced Christ? God and Mary. But the devil also produced a lot of rabbis. *Rebbeleh,* I call them. Little rabbis, in Hebrew. *Rabbonish.* Little, or young rabbis.

"On the other hand, there may be some good rabbis. There may be as many as five, living in New Jersey.

"Sometimes, girlfriends were a substitute for my mother, but mostly they were daughter figures. I was the father in the relationship. Susan Wynner was the perfect substitute for my mother. But we lost contact when I graduated from public school. None of my friends attended the same high school as I did. But finally, I had four friends, for about three years. Then I found that I had nothing more to talk about. But at least they introduced me to the interesting hobby of tropical fish. I didn't even know that, before then.

"Deep in my unconscious, I feel superior. I don't have unconscious paranoia; I have *conscious* paranoia. Sometimes I wonder if there isn't a paranoia drug in the food here. The blood of a paranoid, in the supper? But I'm not serious about being inferior. I'm more serious about being superior: a good person. I was satisfied with being ward president at Hillside Psychiatric Hospital. I didn't have to be president of the United States.

"How many lives have I had before this one? I don't know, too many to say. But one day, I may return to my planet. The voices say that I originated on the planet Mars. I was asleep there. Perhaps, I was only a ray. If the body is destroyed at the proper point, I may return to my planet, where I'll be a sleeping baby, or a ray, or something like that … Reduced to a radio signal.

"She said that she can't send me back to my planet now. But someday, at the proper point, when my body is destroyed, I'll return to my planet, where I was asleep."

* * *

Jonah could no longer recall whether the paper he'd signed so reluctantly was for one treatment, as she had assured him, or for a lifetime of shock (a lifetime of shock – just imagine that, gentlemen!). For it was all conveniently razed and blotted from memory. (*Blotto,* gentlemen.) Until he was methodically reduced to a form of cerebral ash. Until only that body of perpetually daunting darkness – the disembodied voices – ushered from his mouth in a relentless cycle of indecipherable, idiosyncratic logic. A broken record of a man, spinning pointlessly and without consequence.

Once again, the attendants wheeled their charge into shock. And Jonah whispered, almost inaudibly, of a love affair. And of being thrown straight down, he said,

upon one's head.

And on that day, he was declared an *outlaw*. An outlaw, whose guards insisted upon exposing his crimes until they were observable through the skin.

Why an outlaw? Probably, for spending such a long time away from home.

* * *

A note addressed:

TO ALL AND SUNDRY

Concerning these pictures, I send my final instruction.

To those who wish to take a husband or wife, present your great object: *Objet d'art.*

Familiarize yourself with the heart of every woman, and desire frequently the seat of their character.

My reason now bids me, *adieu.*

As a map, whenever one can, one must observe people undressed, standing naked before the world. For a man would spend a fortune to conceal his humpback.

And do you know of a fine painter and a pleasing writer? I acknowledge that merit but, on the other hand, these pictures are too large for meetings of *beaux esprits.*

Well, I am very unwell. Weary to spin out deaths, rotten deaths. A considerable estate fell to such a force. What are the connections? Dying of ennui, I resumed my trade and lived happily and unanimously. *Adieu.*

Even during our waking states, we could not avoid such

morbid visions. Memory itself the result of greenish infantile hallucinations. This character mainly determined by mothers: the earliest visual anything.

My little patient. He was in terrible dread of the attraction. A hysterical woman of forty: a vision struggling for expression. One morning, she opened her eyes; she pulled the sheets over his dream. The obvious visual excitation: God the Woman, as a rather sarcastic lady. Excited during the day, and a wish unfulfilled at night.

Quivering wishes,
striving for expression!

Was it all a practical joke? The scene of a crime? A universal panic, with victims? And what of the description of the cry, written in red ink? (I have seen such things, gentlemen.) One cannot discount a woman's throat, draped neatly over a picture frame. Or a heartbeat placed upon a pillow, and badly mutilated. The theory is perhaps amusing but not unprovable.

And my patient? Fatality makes him appear like an ancient seal: an accident of ripe old age. It serves you right for asking. Thoroughly stifled in life, he is asleep now and in peace, hoping to produce a dream. Yet the unconscious prefers to remain unnoticed, and a still closer examination is of no further interest, as several entrepreneurs now simulate the dream.

Lastly, remember: unacquainted with matters of the deceased, a man cannot be informed. In the end, few have penetration enough of their own work. But with the proper air, with the correct tone, that work may be perfected at last.

Ask questions until you are thoroughly informed of it.

Happy man, fund of parts,
enough to make him bubble!
Great spirits, come walk
and address the ungrateful
young fellows.

* * *

Thus ends Dr. Pluss's FINAL LETTER TO HIS PATIENTS, to whom he bids:

ADIEU.

Rob Couteau's *Doctor Pluss* and *Collected Couteau*:

An essay by Jim Feast, originally published in the *Evergreen Review*

Reading *Doctor Pluss*, Rob Couteau's intense, dramatic story of a psychologist who works at the Walt Whitman Asylum for Adults, one might think, especially since there is no authorial information given on the book, that Couteau is a psychiatrist of some sort. How else could he write with such assurance about this milieu?

However, turning to his book of essays, poems, reviews, and interviews, *Collected Couteau*, though it, too, contains no authorial information, one begins to see that he is a well-informed layman, who has thought deeply about psychological issues. Not only has he thought, but he has also forged a coherent philosophy through both the direct study of the subject and a close reading of literature.

Part of his philosophy is revealed in the interpretation of schizophrenia in a review of a book by John Perry. He notes that "Perry's work in traditional psychiatric settings led him to conclude that those in the thrall of an acute psychotic episode are rarely listened to or met on the level of their visionary state of consciousness." If care providers paid heed to what the patients were trying to show in their symptoms and musings, they would often find that, "forced to live an emotionally impoverished life, the psyche had reacted by provoking a transformation in the form of a 'compensating' psychosis, during which a drama in depth was enacted, forcing the initiate to undergo certain developmental processes."

Couteau quotes Perry concerning this state: "The individual [patient] finds himself living in a psychic modality quite different from his surroundings. He is immersed in a myth world." This modality may seem to be regressive, but it is far from unfruitful. "Although the [myth] imagery is of a general, archetypal nature," writes Couteau, "it also symbolizes the key issues of the individual undergoing the crisis. Therefore, once lived through on this mythic plane, and once the process of withdrawal nears its end, the images must be linked to specific problems of daily life." This leads, in the best cases, to a healing whereby the patient is now able to face and cope with problems that caused the flight into illness.

Perry's work is not that well known, but readers may be more familiar with the once celebrated theories of R. D. Laing. While not finding archetypes in his patients' thoughts, Laing agreed with Perry in treating the schizophrenics' attempts to communicate as valid efforts to reach out, and in finding that their psychological difficulties were often rooted in their untenable lives.

This is not to say that Couteau wholeheartedly endorses these ideas of Perry's. That's not the point. Rather, Dr. Pluss, the staff psychiatrist in the novel named after him, does. Instead of coldly and clinically assessing his schizophrenic patients (as dominant psychiatric norms dictate he should), Pluss befriends them, sharing his own passions, such as his love of modernist art, particularly of Paul Klee, in a workshop where the inmates learn to appreciate art as a form of therapy. Further, he listens carefully to them as they exhaustively recount their life views. He may criticize these patients' sometimes outrageous ideas, but he takes them seriously.

The description on the back of the novel states that the book is "based on actual dialogues with schizophrenic patients," something evident from the stories told to Pluss. With a fantasy akin to Freud's famous Rat Man case, one woman thinks a ravenous cat lives in her midsection. That's why she constantly has to eat. Otherwise, the beast, in its craving for food, will begin consuming her internal organs. (In Freud's story, the patient imagines rats gnawing on his friends' buttocks.)

The most significant patient is Jonah, who believes his own mental problems are so tremendously fascinating that, when he engages in a self-analysis (talking to himself), somehow the Viennese master himself comes back to life to eavesdrop. As Jonah tells Dr. Pluss: "And Freud listened to the analysis, glued to his television. He wouldn't eat; he wouldn't sleep; he wouldn't anything." Ironically enough, Jonah's psychoanalysis simply consists of enumerating, without explaining, his own situation. "I'm a patient; this is a hospital. Why am I in a cage?" While this fantasy may not seem terrifically engaging, when not raving Jonah presents thoughtful and provocative comments on religion, other patients, and even on Dr. Pluss, who is himself undergoing a nervous breakdown.

Pluss had been a painter but gave up the arts to devote himself to helping people. Now, as he is increasingly enthralled by some of his patients' mythic visions, he begins painting again. Using notes of his talks with schizophrenics, he recasts their ideas as art. He creates, for instance, a series of paintings on Jonah, who sometimes thinks of his mind as a clockwork. Pluss depicts "Jonah being cured of paranoia at the Bulova Watch Repair School and leaving behind his persecution complex in the grim milieu of the Bulova assembly line."

Couteau has some misgivings about the sympathetic ear approach of Perry. This is suggested by the fact that Pluss goes beyond listening to his patients' stories, gets caught up by them, and eventually seems to go a little mad himself when he quits the sanitarium and disappears. I say "seems" because, mirroring Pluss's dissolution, the narrative strands of the book, which had been tightly wound in the first section that focused closely on Pluss, begin to unravel, with Jonah taking over much of the narrative and becoming a new focal point. This shift of gears can be a bit disorienting as the realism of the opening is partially abandoned, but it does give the reader a chance to see the schizophrenia developing as it gains hold of Pluss's thought processes. Pluss is like the psychiatrist Dr. Dysart in Peter Shaffer's play *Equus*, who begins to doubt his profession, since when a cure succeeded, it often converted a passionate, inspired, if addled person into a normal but dull zombie. Pluss is attracted by the crazed creativity of so many of his charges. Unlike Dysart, though, who confines his admiration to rueful ruminations, Pluss mimics his patients, becoming psychotic in the process.

I mentioned previously that Couteau obtained psychological knowledge not only from studying and from thinking about books on the mind but also by reading literature. Indeed, it is important to note that while Pluss took the ultimately dangerous path of learning from his patients, Couteau has deepened his insights by interviewing great writers, such as Ray Bradbury and Hubert Selby Jr.

These interviews are not simple Q&A's but are interactions with a lot of give and take. The interview with Selby (done for *Rain Taxi*) delves deeply into spirituality and ethics. In a notable passage, Selby remarks, "What we seem to be taught, at least in the Western world, is that we're born with a blank slate, and we have to learn how to get and get.... But no one ever seems to train us in methods of finding out that we already have within us all the things that are valuable: all the treasures. But it's only in the process of giving them away, to somebody else, that we become aware of having them."

This thought seems to follow up on insights brought to bear in *Doctor Pluss*. One reason for the immobilization of so many in psychiatric offices or institutions (according to Couteau and the Shaffer of *Equus*) is that conventional education does not provide tools for people to deal with stress or act in a humanitarian, giving manner, only instructing them on how to get ahead.

I can't help, though, but note that Selby, like Couteau, suggests he has learned from unique individuals, pointing to none other than *Evergreen Review's* own editor, Barney Rosset, for special commendation. In discussing his first novel, *Last Exit to Brooklyn*, which Rosset published, Selby engages in an interchange, beginning with Couteau's question:

> Why was *Last Exit* allowed to be published in the United States in 1964, while *Tropic of Cancer*, which was a much less obscene book – by the classical definition – was banned until just a few years before this?
>
> **Selby**: I think because ... it [*Tropic*] had been banned for many years. You could only smuggle it in and all that sort of stuff. So, it had a different resistance and a different procedure to go through.

> **Couteau**: It had an already established weight, a history that it had to deal with.
>
> **Selby**: Right. Yeah. And, of course, Barney Rosset took care of business and made it possible for a lot of things to happen.

It's nice to see that old debts – Rosset's discovery and championing of Selby's work – are here being repaid, but this also brings me to a final thought on history. Some readers may find Couteau out of date, in that Laing and the antipsychiatry movement to which he belonged are not the household names they were in the 1960s, but they (as represented by Perry) seem to orient and spur the author's fictional and nonfictional excursions. While some may say this current of psychology has been superseded, Couteau has a gone a long way toward showing that it still possesses validity and staying power. How else account for the intellectual freshness, richness, and potency of his novel and essays?

This essay was featured in the *Evergreen Review* while it was still being edited by the legendary literary figure Barney Rosset. Editor in chief of the magazine and former owner of Grove Press, Rosset published authors such as Samuel Beckett, Pablo Neruda, Henry Miller, Jack Kerouac, Kathy Acker, Octavio Paz, Eugene Ionesco, and Jean Genet.

www.ingramcontent.com/pod-product-compliance
Lightning Source LLC
Chambersburg PA
CBHW051928110726
47902CB00002B/453